FRANCISCA AND THE FORGOTTEN

SOLARIS SANTAELLA

Francisca and the Forgotten | October, 2025, 1st ed.

Edited by Joshua Smyser
Book Design by A.B. Hale
Cover Design by Finny

Published by
Blue Feathered Quill LLC
Evans, Colorado, USA

ISBN-13:
eBook: 978-1-965492-08-6
Paperback: 978-1-965492-09-3
Hard Cover: 978-1-965492-10-9

FRANCISCA AND THE FORGOTTEN

by Solaris Santaella

Content Warning

This book contains depictions of suicide, transphobia, and abuse. Reader discretion is advised, and resources are provided on page 153.

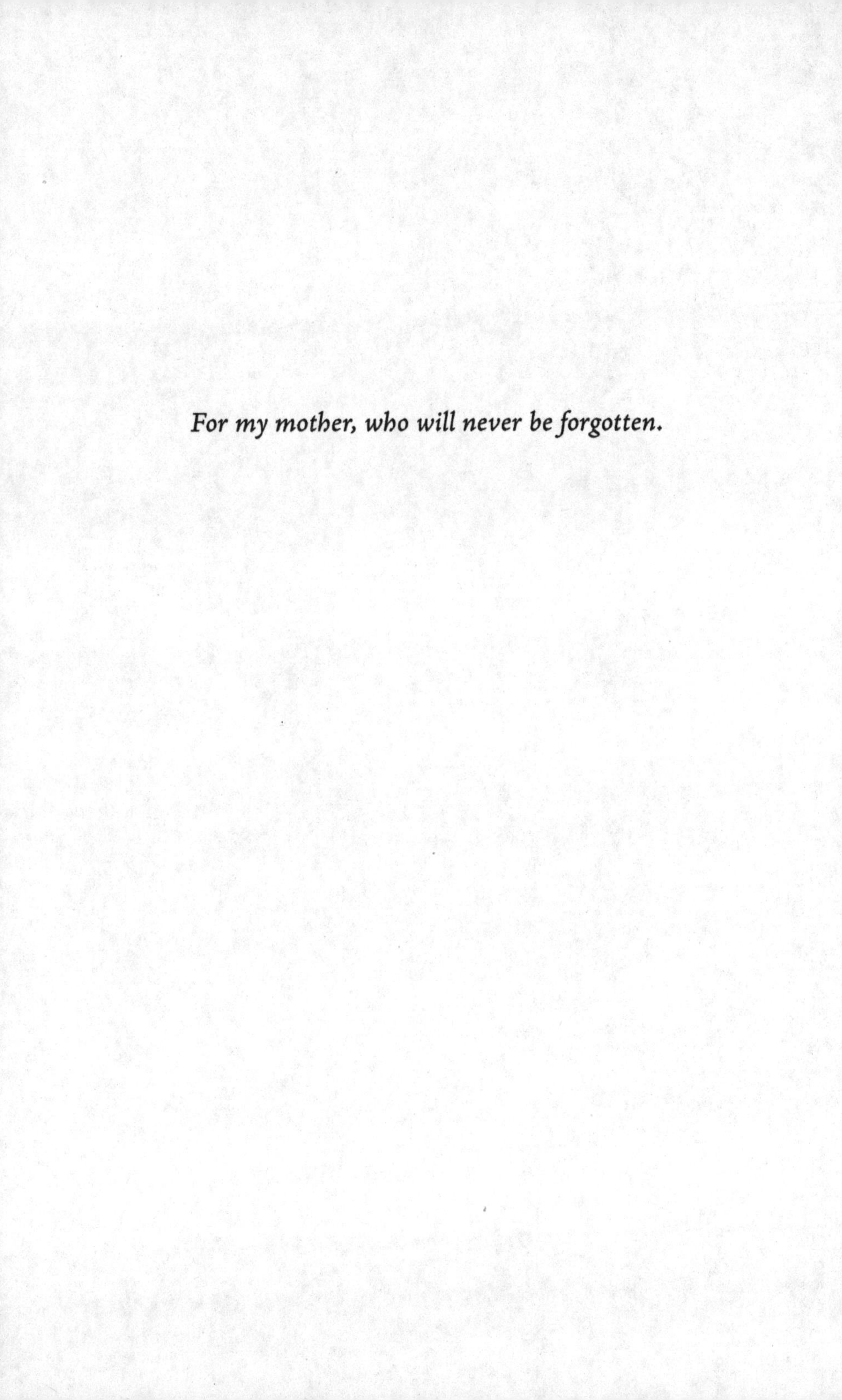

For my mother, who will never be forgotten.

PART ONE:

VIVA

Chapter One

That rotting bird body in the shadow of the orange tree. I don't know if it's a bad omen or what, but it's got to go.

The bird's left wing is bent like a hand stretching skyward, fingers splayed. I see my own hand reflected in its empty eyes. It looks like someone reaching toward me from the bottom of a black pool, waiting to pull me in.

That's when a girl whispers my name.

Francisca.

I pull back, my neck jerking upward. The voice sounded like it was coming from above, but there's no one in the tree. Of course there isn't. No one here even *knows* my name, except my dad. Not that he uses it.

Even though it's summer and you'd think the tree would be thriving, its leaves are dryish and yellowed. They rustle and scrape in the wind. That must have been what I heard. Unless I'm going crazy. Two days trapped in the car with my dad could do that to anyone.

Still, I glance across the street, just in case. There's nothing but cracked streets and faded stucco houses with weedy lawns. This is the historic part of town, so they're all old, like ours, with the same red-tile roofs. Most of them have tiles missing, like gap teeth in the mouths of leering old men.

The chirpy gringa estate lawyer who called us about this dump when my dad's granduncle third time removed or second great-cousin Paco Something Fuentes kicked the bucket described it as "a perfectly charming Mission house." Maybe it had been charming in the

1820s, when it was originally built. As of July 9, 2010, the only mission in my mind is getting as far away as possible. At least I only have a couple years until college.

Ugh. I hate looking on the bright side. It feels like I'm trying to copy my oh-so-perfect older sister Maria Elena.

I roll my eyes. She'd never be caught dead in this situation. If she pointed the bird out to Dad, like I did as he pulled onto the driveway, he'd have picked it up himself instead of going, "So?" Or maybe she'd have launched into one of those dumb Disney songs she sings at pageants, and the bird would've fluttered back to life, tweeting in perfect harmony. Maria Elena would be back inside whipping up a casserole for the neighbors by now.

With my luck, this will probably be the first time any of them see me. I look ridiculous, all gross and sweaty from the car ride, carrying a garbage bag with hands swaddled in bubble wrap. We haven't unpacked the dish gloves yet, and no *way* am I touching that bird barehanded.

My best friend Angie probably would. She was super into dissecting that frog in biology last year, and she collects bugs—the creepier and crawlier, the better. We joke that she should have been born a boy instead of me. She'd have had more fun.

Wind picks up, a welcome relief from the awful dry heat, ruffling my cropped curls. Dad keeps my hair ruthlessly short, but long hair would have been a nuisance. More surface area for sweat to stick to? No thanks. With the shade of the tree, as well as the shadow cast by my trusty black sun hat, it's almost cool.

I bet that bird corpse would smell even worse if it wasn't. It probably already smells like a five-star buffet to any coyotes in the area.

"Here, birdie, birdie, birdie," I mutter under my breath. I stretch the garbage bag toward it, my scarred hands jittering inside their cocoon of bubble wrap. I'm not scared—I just shake a lot. It happens. I had a bad fall off a bike. Whatever.

Up close, I see red ants swarming over the bird's ruffled gray feathers. Great. Even Angie's not crazy enough to collect fire ants. I curl my toes, regretting having worn flip-flops, but shuffle closer anyway.

I grit my teeth and lunge forward, sweeping the bird into the bag. I jump back to avoid the ants. A few of them race up the inside of the bag as I struggle to tie it with my bubble-wrapped hands.

Then I realize there's no need for the bubble wrap anymore, so I shuck my makeshift mitts off, toss them in the bag, and knot it tight.

As I'm looking for a trash can, the front door creaks open. My dad shouts my deadname.

"Let's get cracking and start unpacking!"

His false cheeriness makes me roll my eyes. "In a second!" I holler, lifting the garbage bag.

When he sees that I'm actually doing something, not just blowing him off, Dad grunts and lumbers back inside. That's because the drive'd kept him sober. If he'd been drinking, it wouldn't matter if I was out here helping an orphaned puppy with three legs cross the street—he'd grab my wrist and haul me in. Drunk Dad gets what he wants, or else.

Or else doesn't happen often. Just often enough.

I find a trash can and finally get rid of that dead bird. Then I head inside.

"Bienve-freakin'-nidos, chica," I mutter to myself. "Welcome home."

My dad has his back to me as he rips a box open. I wince at the sound of cardboard tearing, clearing the expression away when he turns to face me. I don't feel like being teased for how sensitive I am.

We spend the afternoon unloading box after box in the ninety-degree heat, which, believe me, is every bit as fun as it sounds. A couple times, Dad tries to make conversation, but since there's little overlap in the things I like to talk about—Mexican rock bands, slam poetry, myths and legends—and the things he likes to talk about—football, *Family Feud*, why the gay agenda is destroying this country—it doesn't go very well. Before long we settle into a silence thick as the dust that coats every surface of the house.

By the time the sun starts setting, we've transferred all the boxes inside. I'm exhausted. I just want to get my room unpacked as quickly as possible and go to bed, but of course Dad has other plans.

"I've already carried your sister's boxes upstairs," Dad tells me. "I'll return the rental trailer and pick us up something for dinner while you take care of Maria Elena's room."

"She doesn't even *live* here!" I explode. I immediately clench my jaw, annoyed at myself for the outburst. There's no point in getting mad at my dad. Nothing I say matters, so I might as well shut up and not embarrass myself.

"Don't you want your sister to have a nice room to come home to when she visits?" Dad's tone makes it clear that the question has only one answer.

"Uh-huh," I sigh, although Maria Elena could sleep in a pit of rattlesnakes for all I care.

I tramp upstairs. Maria Elena's boxes are in the larger of the two bedrooms. Does she have to get *everything*? It's not enough that she inherited our mom's beauty, brains, and social talents while I got—what? The sense of humor? She's also Dad's favorite. No surprise she gets the bigger room.

When my sister started at UT Austin last year, she left enough junk behind to fill a house of her own, but, at our new place, Little Miss Perfect will have to make do with a single spare room. Boo hoo. I'm surprised Dad didn't give her both bedrooms and stick me in the basement or something. All I need now is an organ and I could be the Phantom of the Opera.

I guess that's one thing I got from Mom—musical talent. Not that it does me any good now. I haven't touched my violin in years.

I hear Dad's rusting wreck sputter to life, then he peels off. With how he drives—blasting through every red light, blowing past stop signs, getting into stupid races every time a bigger truck pulls up next to him—it's a wonder we made it to Claudesville in one piece.

I hate riding with him. Even though I'm the bad kid in the family, I honestly don't even jaywalk when I'm alone. There are plenty of rules I have no problem breaking, but, usually, the price for breaking them isn't getting hit by a car and, you know, *dying*.

There are times dying doesn't seem all that bad, but it'd have to be on my own terms. If I made a list of ways it could happen, death-by-car wouldn't crack the top ten. Too messy.

I don't think Dad will be back for a while. Knowing him, he won't return with dinner before he's found the nearest place to blow a paycheck in one sitting. I grit my teeth. It's Dad's fault we had to move here, his gambling debts that forced him to sell our family home in San Antonio.

I knew every inch of that house, even the spider-infested crawl space I used to sneak into during games of hide and seek. I knew which steps creaked the loudest—the first two, I always jumped to avoid them—and which burners on the stove made weird popping sounds before the gas turned on. The thought of facing a completely different house makes me anxious, which annoys me. More than that, I hate having to leave the place where I grew up, where I learned to ride a bike and play violin, where we scattered the ashes of our old bulldog, Brisket.

The last place I saw my mother.

I remember the porch out front where we used to sit together. She'd be smoking a cigarette, and the diamond on her wedding ring would flash as she lifted her hand to her mouth. Then she'd flick the butt into a can of Diet Coke—she pretty much always had at least one empty can nearby—and wipe her long-nailed hands down the front of her tight-fitting jeans. I used to lay on my back, my head next to her red cowboy boots, and sing.

My eyes threaten to tear up. I get that she had to get away from Dad and all, but I just wish I could call her. It's been years since I've heard her voice. She used to send emails, but even those dried up a while back. Something must have happened to her—something horrible, something that forced her to drop off the grid—but as soon as everything clears up, she'll find me again. She has to. I know she's missing me just as much as I miss her.

My chest tightens. I can't breathe in this stupid, dusty house, surrounded by boxes of my sister's stuff. I don't know where I can go, but I've got to get out. I run downstairs and turn a corner, finding myself face to face with the screen covering the back door. I pull it open and step outside, forcing myself to breathe deeply.

The backyard is just sand, shrubs, and a sad cluster of faded sun-flowers over by the fence. True to their name, they're turned toward the setting sun, away from me. Gradually, I calm down, and my hand slips into the pocket of my cargo shorts, pulling out my flip phone. I might not be able to call my mom, but I can do the next best thing.

I call Tia Lola.

"How fast can you get to California?" I ask.

She laughs, but her low voice is sympathetic when she says, "That bad, huh?"

I glance back inside the house. A cockroach scurries along the wall.

"You have no idea." I sigh. "Any cool poetry slams this weekend?"

"Aren't there always?" Tia Lola replies.

Tia Lola took me to my first poetry slam when I was twelve, at a café one of her friends worked at. It was nothing like all the boring recitations Maria Elena did, with one performer standing stiffly on the stage in formal clothes, spitting out someone else's words.

Slam poetry felt *alive*. Poets shouted and moved, and the audience snapped, cheered, and booed the judges for giving out scores too low. One of the poets, an older woman with long purple locs, jumped onto our table as she screamed out her final lines. I stared at her scuffed combat boots, hooked. I tried to get a spoken word club started back in middle school, but the teacher who let us use her classroom during lunch made us leave when she caught me standing on her desk.

I wonder if the high school here has a spoken word club. My old one did. It was run by Ms. Andrews, who'd probably taught 10th grade English to pterodactyls. She didn't like my table-jumping ways either, but she wasn't all bad. She used to tell us that everything you observe is a poem waiting to be written.

Yeah, right. What about when there's nothing to observe because everything around you is *boring?* Take those stupid sunflowers bobbing in the wind. They look like every set of sunflowers you've ever seen. My eyes keep falling back on them because there's nothing else to look at in the yard. Instead, I shift my gaze to the sky, which is a streaky salmon color.

There's a muffled voice on my aunt's end. "Dolores says to tell you the regulars miss you already."

Dolores Delgacio is Tia Lola's partner of twelve years and my mentor in all things butch. I've known her practically all my life. She's like a second aunt, or the cool older sister I wish I had instead of the thoroughly lame one I actually got. I might never have realized I was trans without her.

If my only options were to be a boy or become a girl like my sister, I'd have been miserable either way. I've got nothing against girlie-girls—just ask my friend Cat, who squeals at the sight of Angie's bugs and would rather drop dead than go a day without sparkly pink lip gloss. I just never wanted to be one.

But Dolores—she and the other regulars at Tia Lola's with their work boots, tool belts, and ladies' names tattooed on their arms showed me everything a woman could be. I wanted to be like that: tough yet tender, someone who put their arms around a femme and made her feel safe. I didn't want to look polished, or preppy, or, God forbid, *straight*.

I know Dolores's schedule backwards and forwards, which is why it's a surprise to find out that she's at the tattoo parlor so early.

"It's past seven," Tia Lola tells me.

"Oh, right." I realize they're now two hours ahead of me.

An ache of longing fills my chest. I wish I was sitting on the black and white checkered counter in Tia Lola's tattoo parlor, waiting for one of her friends to deal the next hand. It's Friday night, which means Texas hold 'em. Saturdays it's blackjack, and Sundays Dad doesn't let me go over because we have family dinner, which is like every other dinner, except Maria Elena happens to grace us with her presence. I guess me and Dad don't count as a family without her. Somehow, it's still supposed to count without Mom.

Tia Lola, who knows me better than anyone, says softly, "We wish you were here, too, chica."

I choke out a goodbye and hang up before I can start crying. I keep my head tipped upward for a long time, until the threat of tears falls away. I take a deep, shaky breath and allow my chin to drop. Then my stomach drops.

The sunflowers are staring at me.

Okay, so not *staring*-staring. They don't have eyes or anything, thank god. They're just…facing me.

Not the sun. Me.

The same flowers I was bored with moments before. Nothing special about them. There's no reason for me to be scared.

I want to turn away, but I can't. It feels too much like I'm being watched, like the dark center of each flower has its own malicious intelligence. I'm reminded of the dead bird's eyes. I can almost see a faint hand reaching toward me—

I close my eyes tight. When I open them again, the sunflowers are facing the fence.

Okay, so I'm hallucinating. Great. I must have had too many energy drinks on the drive over. That, and my dad stopping at every Dairy Queen between here and San Antonio has given me the mother of all sugar highs. No wonder I'm jittery. Plus, there's the stress of moving to a new place. And the wind. Can't forget the wind. It was messing with that orange tree in the front yard, too. I let out a long sigh and edge backward into the house, locking the door for good measure.

The sunflowers stay put.

Chapter Two

I head back upstairs to finish unpacking Maria Elena's room. Before long, it looks like a picture from a catalog, all matchy-match, with a maroon bedspread, fuzzy rugs, and curtains. I prop a couple mannequin heads wearing curly brunette wigs and old rhinestone crowns up on her white vanity and decorate the walls. Didn't it occur to Dad that there's a *reason* she left this stuff behind? Obviously not, so here I am, pinning posters of boy bands she probably doesn't even like anymore up alongside Italian landscape puzzles she and Dad did together years ago.

When I'm done, I peer out the window. My dad's truck is nowhere in sight. My stomach rumbles. I hope he hurries back with the food, then I hope it's Taco Bell. I might be Mexican, but I'm also half white, and I'm pretty sure that half is one hundred percent concentrated in my tongue since I have zero tolerance for spicy food and can't roll my R's.

Since I have time, I head over to the smaller bedroom: mine. It's across from Maria Elena's and up the hall from the spare room Dad plans to use as an office. What he needs an office for when he's unemployed, I don't know.

My room has pink tile floors and wallpaper that's either supposed to be pale yellow or dark beige. The window looks out on the orange tree I noticed earlier. Shriveled fruits cling to withered branches, so close to the window I could reach out and pluck one, if they didn't look disgusting.

My room's a lot easier to unpack since Dad made me sell most of my belongings in a yard sale before we moved. Mostly clothes, mostly in black. My collection of cheap sunglasses. A few childhood blankets too ratty to sell off, folded up and piled in a squat, woven bamboo hamper. A poorly put-together bookshelf that leans to the side. Torn, dog-eared paperbacks, most of them stained by splotches of orange soda since I spilled a Fanta while I was packing up.

There are three possessions that mean more to me than all the others put together: my violin, the dollhouse, and my parent's wedding picture.

I haven't played the violin in years. Since it's a half-size, I can't even use it anymore, but I couldn't bear to give it up. I lied and told my dad I lost it when he told me to bring it out for the yard sale.

The dollhouse, I couldn't hide, but, strangely enough, it didn't sell. The wicked glares I directed at any hopeful child that so much as glanced in its direction might have had something to do with that. It's an old white Victorian manor with one of the gables smashed in where my dad kicked it after I got a C in fifth grade math. I'm too old to play with it anymore, but it was a gift from my abuela, may she rest in peace.

The wedding picture is a thing of beauty. It has a heart-shaped frame of frosted glass, and it feels cool and heavy in your hands, important. My mom's laughing face takes up most of the picture, but my father's there, too—slimmer and less whiskery, smiling. They look like a fairytale prince and princess, even though I know there's no happy ending. A few weeks after Mom went missing, I crept into the bedroom that used to be hers and took the picture from the bedside table so I'd never forget what she looks like. I want to recognize her when she comes back. I don't think Dad ever noticed.

I tuck the violin case under my bed, set the dollhouse up along the opposite wall next to a stack of boxes I'm too lazy to break down, then open the last package, grimacing at the tearing sound as I rip the tape off in one long strand. I wrapped the picture up as carefully as I could using the cherry red silk dress Maria Elena wore to her junior prom and put it on top. The dress stands out against my band tees and ripped jeans like a neon warning sign.

I'll say this for my sister—she might not understand the whole transgender thing, or the lesbian thing, or the transgender lesbian thing that is Francisca Luna Fuentes, but she tries. She gave me the dress when I came out to her two years ago. It was a sweet gesture, even though I'd never be caught dead at a school dance. Besides, it makes great packing material.

Just as I'm setting the glass frame carefully on top of my dresser, Dad appears in the doorway, greasy fast food bags in hand. His eyes narrow at the wedding picture, and I brace myself for a fight.

"I know you miss her, but you can't let that control your whole life," he says almost gently. "You need to move on."

My face burns. Even I can't tell if it's with shame or anger. Maybe both.

"It doesn't," I grit out. "And she'll come back one day. I know it."

How could my mother leave when every memory I have of her is so full of love, it hurts? I remember her playing dolls with me for hours, even when Dad insisted I play with something more masculine. I remember when I lost my favorite stuffed animal, a turtle named Girdle, at the YMCA during swimming lessons and she let me stay home from school the next day to cry it out, bringing me blankets and ginger ale like I was sick. I remember her lilting laugh ringing out over the sound of pins getting knocked down when I bowled my first strike. I remember her gentle hand on my back as she taught me how to ride a bike.

There has to be a reason she left; she never would have abandoned me if she didn't have to. She loved me.

Loves me. Present tense.

Dad must realize that we're making history here, getting through an entire day without a full-on scream fight, because he doesn't say a word. He just holds out a smushed cheeseburger like the world's saddest, greasiest peace offering. I take it because I'm too worn down to fight and follow him downstairs.

Dinner's subdued, silent except for our muffled chewing. We eat at the foot of the stairwell, not bothering to walk to the dining room. Even though nothing bad happened between us today, I'm reminded of a hundred other meals that sat heavy in my stomach after he yelled at me. That's one thing I can say about Dad—he's never too upset to eat. Who knows how many excruciating tirades he's wrapped up with a reminder that I need to eat some cookies to get rid of the milk before it expires, or that he picked up cupcakes on the way home from work?

Once Dad finishes his meal, he digs his cell phone out of the pocket of his army-green cargo pants and opens it.

"Let's call your sister."

I roll my eyes but, the truth is, I'm grateful for the suggestion. Talking to Maria Elena might not be my idea of a good time, but it beats sitting around and staring at the floor.

Dad punches in my sister's number, holding the phone between us so we can both hear. Maria Elena picks up on the first ring, because of course she does.

"Hi, Dad!" she chirps. I picture her ponytail swinging over her shoulder as she talks, her big red cheerleader bow bouncing. She looks like a second-grader on picture day most of the time, except during pageants, when she breaks out the red lipstick and false eyelashes and padded bras. "How's the new house?"

Dad burps and tosses a wadded-up burger wrapper onto the ground. "It's a work in progress."

I groan and lean down to pick up his trash. This place is enough of a dump without adding literal garbage to the equation. "He means it sucks," I translate, tossing his wrapper into the paper bag where I'm keeping my trash.

"I'm sure it's not *that* bad," says Maria Elena.

"How would you know?" I snap. "You're not here!"

"That's enough from you," says my dad in a warning tone.

I shake my head, but I don't say another word.

Dad asks Maria Elena how class is going—she's taking a communications elective and Italian over the summer—and she says it's *sooo* amazing, and she's meeting *sooo* many cool people, and I *sooo* want to rip my ears off. Maybe silence was better after all.

She and Dad talk for a while, and I head to the kitchen to get rid of the trash. The kitchen's oddly long and narrow, and in places the plaster on the walls is flaking off, revealing dingy-looking brick. I open a cabinet, more out of boredom than genuine curiosity, and find nothing but cracked wood, dust, and cobwebs since we haven't unpacked the plates and silverware yet. Without bothering to close it, I turn back toward the trash can.

Crack!

Something like a gunshot rings out behind me. I jump, then hate myself for jumping. It's just the cabinet door. But tell that to my racing heart.

I glance over my shoulder to confirm that, obviously, some freak with a gun didn't manifest behind me. Sure enough, I'm alone, and the cabinet is closed. It slammed shut so hard, the old wood has started to splinter. Note to self—old things break easy.

I head back for the stairs, intending to go up and finish unpacking my room, but Dad intercepts me, holding out the phone. "She wants to talk to you."

I take the phone with a sigh. "Yeah?"

"I know you weren't very excited about the move, but look on the bright side," says Maria Elena, "at least you're moving right before the start of the school year. It'll be a fresh start."

"Lucky me," I say bitterly. "I get hauled off halfway across the country to start school as the weird kid no one knows."

And it's not like I'm great at winning people over, either. Cat and Angie, they've been my friends since we were eating graham crackers and throwing Legos at each other at daycare. I haven't made a new friend since, unless you count the lesbians Tia Lola plays cards with. I do, but since teachers always bring up my "social development" at parent-teacher conferences, I guess they don't.

"Well, my point was, it was going to be an adjustment either way," Maria Elena replies. "I think it would have been so much harder to move if you were already settled into a routine."

She's right, but I'm mad at her for making me agree, for being sympathetic when I'm trying to hate her. No matter how nice she is, I have to keep reminding myself that it's not real, none of it. It's a performance. It's all part of her grand plan to be the perfect sibling, the one that gets all the attention, praise, and love.

I sigh through my nose. I know, deep down, that's not true, but I kind of wish it was, that way I wouldn't have to feel so guilty about how angry Maria Elena makes me.

To calm myself down, I make a mental list of all the ways Maria Elena isn't so perfect. She failed pre-calc her junior year of high school. She picks her nose when she thinks no one's looking. She borrows my books without asking, and the fact that she usually returns them before I even know they're gone means *nothing* because she should've kept her hands off them in the first place. She says "*sooo*," like, sooo much more than she should.

My favorite memory, though, is of the time I pranked her one night during a sleepover with her friends when she was in middle school. I snuck into her room after all the giggling died down and stuck her hand into a bowl of warm water, making her pee the bed. She smacked the hell out of me, and Mom and Dad didn't even punish her for it, but it was worth it. At least, that's what I thought at the time, but Maria Elena got me back good when she embarrassed me in front of my second-grade class by announcing that I still slept with a Buzz Lightyear night light. Then she smiled sweetly as everyone laughed and pretended she had no idea why I was angry-crying the whole way home.

"Just remember," she told me, pausing to blow a bubble with her gum. *Crack.* Not that I'd ever tell her, but I kind of liked the sound; it reminded me of getting a strike at the bowling alley. "You can start fights all you want, but I'll finish them."

That incident showed me that, underneath the nicey-nice exterior, Maria Elena can be just as mean, and messy, and human as I am. When I remember that, I almost kind of like her.

Once our conversation wraps up, I give Dad his phone and I head upstairs to finish unpacking my room. Almost everything's out of the boxes, but there's some pictures I need to tack up. Before I get to work, I slip my MP3 player out of the backpack pocket I kept it zipped in and put on my favorite song. Guitar and violin notes caress me at once, and a warm, gorgeous voice croons my name. I sing along.

"*Francisca,*" sings Citadel Sanchez, lead vocalist of Luna Del Sol. The violin picks up; I can just picture Luna Lallevera sawing away at her neon blue electric violin, attacking every triplet note.

"*Quieres llevar montañas por mano,*
Quieres cuentar las estrellas solá."

"*Solá,*" a lower voice echoes, harmonizing with Citadel's. It's Sol Estevez, guitarist and backup vocalist.

In spite of everything, the music almost makes me feel better. Almost.

I let the song play on as I set my one stick of eyeliner, a half-empty bottle of Bloody Mary nail polish, my mom's favorite shade of red, and a pair of cat-eye sunglasses on my desk. Then I tape up a bulldog of the month calendar and some pictures: a strand from the photo booth at the mall I took with Angie and Cat after a middle school bowling tournament, a few pictures of Brisket dozing off, a candid of my mother. She's smiling in the sunlight with a feathery dandelion in hand, ready to make a wish.

Sighing, I wipe sweat off my forehead. I could really use a cold shower, but I can hear the water running from here—there's only one bathroom, and Dad's using it. Instead, I open the bottle of nail polish, thinking I'll paint my nails to give myself a break from unpacking, but there's just enough chipped black polish left on them that I decide against it. Then I open the window to try and coax in some coolness. The orange tree's leaves are stirring slightly in the night air, so I figure there must be a breeze.

I watch the leaves rustle, then glance down to the roots, where I found the dead bird. I feel for it, honestly. I bet it had a bird-family once, parent-birds for sure, probably at least one sister-bird. Maybe the sister-bird had brighter feathers and a prettier singing voice, and after the mother-bird went missing, the father-bird tried to fill the void by signing the older sister-bird up for bird beauty pageants, and she was always winning, bringing back little crowns fitted for her tiny birdie head while the younger sister-bird stayed behind in the nest, alone. Or something.

Despite the leaves continuing to wave, the room doesn't seem to get any colder. It's like the wind stops just short of the house. I glance out the window. While a few neighboring yards have trees of their own, their branches are still. There must be something strange about the way this street is set up for only our house to be affected by the wind like this, or maybe the orange tree just has thinner branches.

I hear the water shut off and head for the bathroom. Fresh from the shower, I'm busy dumping my clothes in the hamper when a gust of air rushes past me, rifling through the photos I just taped up. The one of my mother flutters to the desk. As I rush to pick it up, I accidentally bump the still-open bottle of nail polish. It soaks the thin paper, bleeding through my mother's face. I stare at the spreading puddle of red, too numb to even cry.

At least I still have the wedding picture. I touch the cool glass, my mother's laughing face, and for a moment, nothing feels as bad. I can't bring myself to throw the ruined picture away, though. I just leave it there to dry, not knowing what I'll do after that.

I sigh heavily. With that shower out of the way, there's nothing keeping me from going to bed. Might as well try and get some sleep.

The orange tree has other plans.

I forgot to close the window, so I can hear every crackle of dry leaves, every murmur of the wind. It's annoying. At first. Then the tree starts speaking to me.

Francisca, Francisca!

A girl's voice again, but different from earlier—brighter. It sounds like a friend calling me to play.

A child murmurs, "*Mamá?*"

"*Girasol*," sighs an old man.

I might not have grown up speaking Spanish at home, but I was raised around enough people who did to pick up a thing or two. *Girasol* means sunflower. I recall the sunflowers in the backyard and shiver.

That's it—I'm closing the window.

I wrap my trembling fingers around the splintery windowpane. Up close, I see the glass is scratched, probably from the tree branches scraping against it. Wind blasts me in the face. Dead leaves come crumbling off the tree and into my room. I gag at the reek of rotting fruit. The oranges loom closer than ever. In the moonlight, their wrinkled skins almost look like flesh.

I slam the window shut. Just before it closes, the wind thrusts a spindly branch forward. The window comes down like a guillotine. *Snap!*

A shriveled brown finger falls to the floor. Before I can even scream, I realize it's just a broken twig.

I suck down air, trying to force myself to calm down. What is with me today? I must be even more tired than I thought. With the window closed, I drop into bed, fully prepared to sleep like a rock.

Of course that doesn't happen.

Chapter Three

It doesn't start off like a nightmare.

You know how in dreams, you sometimes see yourself from the outside, and you don't look like yourself, but you still recognize it as you? Maybe you look like your favorite actress or a character from a TV show. In this dream, I look like a girl I can't quite place.

Dream-me is dressed like she's Amish or something, with a floor-length black skirt and starched white blouse partially covered by a black mantilla. My features are more delicate, my skin a slightly darker brown. My hair is long and wavy, deep brown instead of black, and it's plaited. A sunflower is tucked behind my ear. I'm smiling, and even though that smile looks nothing like my crooked one, it's *my* smile. I feel it and see it at the same time because dreams are weird like that.

I also see my sister. Maria Elena's dressed all ye olde, too, and she looks younger—closer to fourteen than nineteen—but other than that, she's about right. Same glossy curls, full lips, and the narrow but hooked nose that sometimes loses her points at pageants, sometimes gets away with being "exotic." We don't look much alike, in this dream or outside of it, but we do have the same nose.

There's also an old man with a face dotted by moles—my abuelo. In real life, my abuelo died before I was born, but, in the dream, being with him is the most natural thing in the world. He and Maria Elena are squatting by a riverbank, and I'm standing further back, watching from a field of sunflowers, gathering a bouquet.

I hear Abuelo call my sister "Mariposa", and I notice flowers of all shapes and sizes scattered around her feet, spilling out of a big leather satchel. That's right—she's Mariposa, always fluttering from flower to flower, unable to choose which one she likes best. She has oleanders in her hair, and I have a daisy chain she wove for me around my wrist. I'm Giri, Girasol, because I bring Abuelo sunflower bouquets from the field between our houses whenever I visit.

I watch my sister and grandfather gather stones.

"Ay, mija, it's all I can do to lift myself out of bed. If I try to pick up one of those heavy rocks, I'll break my poor old wrist," Abuelo jokes.

Maria Elena laughs. "Liar. You know you're the only one who can give me a challenge."

"If you let your sister practice—" Abuelo begins.

"Oh, she doesn't want to skip stones," said Maria Elena with a careless toss of her curls. "She's busy picking flowers. Isn't that right?" she calls.

"Right!" I call back, beaming and holding up my bouquet.

My awake-self stirs beneath the surface of the dream. I want to tell Maria Elena where she can stick her stones, but the impulse fades fast. She's my sister, after all. I love her. I'm happy just to watch.

Maria Elena puckers her mouth, eyes narrowed in concentration as she throws the first stone. She's strong, but she has no strategy. Her stone goes far, but the second it strikes the water's surface, it sinks. Abuelo tosses a stone lightly, and it skips on and on.

"Again," Maria Elena demands.

Abuelo laughs. "Serious things, you treat like games, and games, you take so seriously! What if I refuse to play? What then?"

Maria Elena just smiles at him as the skin sloughs off her face.

Then I'm sitting with Abuelo in the shaded arcades of his house, saying nothing. I have sunflowers in my hands, but I pass them over without speaking, and he takes them with a heavy sigh. He doesn't call me Giri anymore. We both know why. Every time, all we could think about was Maria Elena and the sunflower sentinels standing tall around her grave.

"Lonely, isn't it?" he murmurs, his heavy hand on my head. "It's lonely for a flower with no mariposa."

I feel lonely with him right beside me. He was always more Maria Elena's grandfather than mine. Without her, I've lost him, too. We're both lost.

I'm going home through the sunflower field, but it stretches on forever, and the sky is black above me. Not just night-black, but starless. Yet somehow I can still see my mother, cradling a sunflower in her arms like a baby, watching me with flashing eyes. Then she vanishes.

I hear crying—mine?—as sunflower stems entwine around me, pulling me into the earth. I struggle, but they wrap around me too tightly, binding my limbs, digging into my flesh. I gasp for air but gag on petals. I'm dragged down deeper and deeper. Skulls grin at me from all directions, all but glowing in the dark. There's my mom, there's Abuelo, there's Maria Elena—they're dead, all of them, and I have no choice but to join them. I'm no one without them. I'm being buried alive.

I wake up face down, suffocating on my pillow. I jolt upright, wipe drool off my mouth, and try to shake off the dream weirdness. Even though I showered just before bed, I feel grimy all over, like I'm still covered in dirt. I run my hands over my arms, looking for marks left by those sunflowers. Stupid. There's just some faint imprints from my bunched-up sheets.

Still. I'm not taking my chances.

I slip downstairs, careful not to wake Dad, and open the back door as slowly as possible to keep it from creaking. The sun is barely rising, so the light is weak. Even so, I can easily make out the wall's dark silhouette, and I know the sunflowers are all in one corner.

I race across the yard and yank them out of the ground, one by one. Dry earth crumbles away from thin roots. Loose petals cascade down, tickling my toes. I jump like I'm dodging ants. Then I throw the flowers over the fence. There's just a torn up patch of dirt where they used to grow, like a freshly dug-up grave. I shudder.

Goodbye, freaky flowers. I know, logically, that there's no connection between those sunflowers and my strange dream, just like I know they didn't *really* look at me last night, but I don't care. I feel better with them gone. Lighter. If only I could do something about that weird, whispering tree up front, but something tells me that's going to be harder to get rid of. I wonder if this town has a hardware store, somewhere I could get ahold of a chainsaw.

I head back to the door only to find it locked behind me. Just my luck. I sigh, leaning my head against the screen. It's early enough in the morning that the metal is soothing and cool instead of scalding hot. What now? I guess there's nothing to do but knock on the front door and hope Dad hears me. I grimace at the prospect. He's not going to be happy if I wake him up too early. I run a hand through my hair, resigning myself to a few boring hours outside. At least it's not as hot as it was yesterday. Yet.

I'm halfway around the house when it occurs to me—I didn't hold the door open when I talked to Tia Lola yesterday. Shouldn't it have locked behind me then, too? Whatever. I must have bumped into a latch on my way out this morning, or something. No need to go around making up mysteries just because I'm still unsettled from that dream.

Speaking of mysteries—I glance up at the front of the house and my window is. Wide. Open. The window I know for *sure* I closed. I can still hear that twig snapping in half. Maybe I went to sleep earlier than I thought and I was already dreaming then? That would explain why the stick looked like a finger for a second.

It's not a satisfying explanation, but what are the alternatives? Either something's seriously wrong with this house, or someone broke in. The second idea cheers me up for a second, but I quickly discard it. There's plenty of windows on the first floor a burglar could've snuck through, and they'd have to be pretty small to climb that orange tree. Those upper branches would probably break if anyone heavier than Maria Elena put weight on them. They'd definitely snap under mine. Too bad, otherwise I could climb into my room.

The tree's branches stir in a wind my skin doesn't feel. Okay, so there are other reasons I wouldn't climb that thing if my life depended on it. Getting yelled at by Dad won't be fun, but it beats breaking my neck or being cursed.

I lean with my back against the front door and sit down, keeping an eye on the tree. I watch it for a while, but there's nothing to see. Gradually, my eyelids droop, and I fall asleep, thankfully without dreaming this time. When I wake up, blinking and disoriented, I squint at the sun. It's still morning, still earlier than Dad will want to be woken up, but I think I can get away with a scolding instead of a scream fit.

I bang on the door for what feels like forever. Eventually, I hear heavy footsteps inside, getting closer, then Dad opens the door.

"What are you *doing* out here?"

It occurs to me I have zero explanation. What am I supposed to say—I had a bad dream, so I got up stupid early and tore up all the flowers in the backyard? I glance back at the tree and remember the dead bird.

"I thought I heard coyotes outside," I lie smoothly. "I went out to check, and the door locked behind me."

"What coyotes?" Dad snaps, rubbing his red eyes. He gestures at the neighborhood around us. "Does this look like the middle of the wilderness to you?"

Just the middle of nowhere, I think.

"You probably heard a neighbor's cat," Dad tells me, stepping aside so I can enter the house. He crosses his arms, snorting and shaking his head. "Dragged out of bed at the crack of dawn over a damned cat…"

When his back is turned, I roll my eyes. The living room clock says it's almost eight-forty-five—hardly "the crack of dawn."

Halfway up the stairs, Dad pauses. Without turning around, he says, "If you're up causing trouble this early, the least you could do is make breakfast."

"How? There's no food in the house," I point out.

"There's a store in town. You can figure it out."

I glance at my dad's car keys, hanging enticingly near the door. "Does that mean I can take the truck?"

A bark of laughter. "You wish."

I stifle a groan. I should've known better than to expect my dad to be *reasonable*, especially while he's still bitter about being woken up. I guess I'll just walk through this strange town alone and defenseless, hoping nobody decides to kidnap me. I half grin. When I was a kid, I used to wish I'd get kidnapped, that way Dad might focus on me instead of Maria Elena. More likely than not, he'd have just been glad to get me off his hands.

I head to my room to change, but I stop before making it to the dresser.

Chapter Four

Oh, *hell* no.

I could just about handle the weird plants, and the windows and doors opening and closing on their own, but I am *not* sticking around while some ghost makes doll dioramas.

Because it has to be ghosts, right? I see that stick from last night—which means I wasn't dreaming when I closed the window—propped up against my dollhouse. That would be weird enough on its own, since I didn't put it there, but that's not all, folks!

No, you see, overnight, that stick seems to have grown from a single twig to a small branch—almost a miniature tree. And in that tree is one of my old dolls. More specifically, the head of one of my dolls. Just the head. Her long brown hair is all tangled in the branches, but her painted-on smile is bright as ever. The rest of the body lies broken at the base of the tree, limbs twisted in impossible positions.

I'm a reasonable girl—I do what anyone would have done. I scream, and scream, and scream.

"This house is haunted!" I shout. It feels good to admit it—I'm not crazy after all! I'm a perfectly normal person who just so happens to live in a horrible ghost house.

At the sound of my voice, the wind in the orange tree, which I've never heard let up for a second, stops. It's like a hush falling on a crowded room, strangers cutting off conversations just to hear me speak. The ghost is listening, as if it's glad I'm finally recognizing its presence.

I only have one thing to say to it.

"I don't know who you are, and I don't care," I announce, shoving clothes into my backpack. "I'm out of here!"

"What are you yelling about?" Dad demands, stopping me in the hallway.

"This house is haunted," I repeat, almost calmly, "but that's fine. I was just leaving."

Dad gives me a suspicious look. He knows I'm weird, and he's used to me mouthing off, but he doesn't know what to make of this. "What do you mean, haunted?"

"We've got ghosts," I reply. "Ghosts, ghouls, maybe some kind of poltergeist. Don't know, don't care. I'm not sticking around long enough to find out."

Dad lets out a long, grumbly breath through his nose. "Look, you want to go back to San Antonio. Tough luck," he says. "This is where we live now."

I hadn't even thought about San Antonio. I would have settled for living anywhere other than here, but, now that he mentions it—

Dad continues. "I'm not dealing with this right now. Get yourself dressed and go to the store."

Right, breakfast. The most important meal of the day. Ghosts might be planning to invade our bodies and wear our skins, but who cares about that when Dad hasn't had his eggs and hot sauce yet? There's no point in arguing with him. I figure I'll go to the store, then call Tia Lola and beg her to take me home. I'll make sure she knows I'm dead serious this time.

I remember passing a Walmart on the drive in, but I don't know how to get there. Fortunately, the town is so small, pretty much everything is located around one main road. It takes some trial and error, and a few wrong turns down dirt roads around the neighborhood, but I eventually make it to the main street. I can't see the Walmart, but if I walk this road long enough, I'll find it.

The rest of the town is dusty and dirt poor, but normal. The only thing that stands out is the library, which is painted white, and it has a big stone square in front of it. I think it's the base of a statue, only there's nothing on top of it. I'm almost curious enough to cross the street to see if there's some kind of plaque, but I stop myself. I'm not staying in this town for a second longer than necessary.

I never make it to the Walmart, but I find a little Mexican place. It's more of a shack than a restaurant, with a metal roof and smoke curling from the windows, and a cardboard sign taped to the door promising "cheap food aquí". It smells like they're cooking breakfast burritos inside, and that's good enough for me. If Dad wants real groceries, he can hop in the truck and buy them himself. I eat my burrito on the walk back, regretting it when I turn down the road to our house. The orange tree's dark branches are waving, and suddenly I feel sick to my stomach.

I give Dad his breakfast, let him complain about the lack of groceries, then go to my room to call Tia Lola. My phone is dead because of course it is, because if anything in life ever went right for me, I wouldn't be Francisca Fuentes. My dad yells at me to unpack his office, so I do that while I wait for the phone to charge. I come back an hour later, and the battery's still at zero.

I groan. Either the charger's broken, or there's a problem with the outlet. Since this house is roughly a billion years old, I wouldn't be surprised if it was the latter. It wouldn't have had outlets when it was originally built. This place must have been redone a dozen times, not that you'd guess from the state of it outside.

I spend the rest of the day drifting from room to room, testing outlets. Some of them work—the computer in my dad's office is up and running, and so is his desk lamp—but my phone refuses to charge. Must be the charger after all.

Although it's the last thing I want to do, I ask my dad if I can borrow his phone.

"What for?" he barks.

"To call Tia Lola," I reply.

He snorts. "You can't be running up the phone bill calling long distance every day. Do you think I'm made of money?"

"Well, my charger's not working. Do we at least have enough money for that?"

Dad shrugs. "Should've said something before I got groceries—I could've picked one up for you. Now you'll have to wait until tomorrow."

I grit my teeth and nod. There's nothing I can do but wait.

I'm on high alert for any ghost activity the rest of the day, but nothing happens. By the time I'm taking my evening shower, I've almost convinced myself that maybe there's nothing going on here after all.

Maybe the stick wasn't smaller last night. I mean, I did also think it looked like a finger. Clearly my eyes weren't the most reliable.

As for the doll, I know I didn't put it there. Could Dad have done it? Not really his style. Ripping the head off a doll, sure, but he wouldn't have put it in the tree, spreading its hair through the branches, placing the limbs just so. Maybe I did do it…in my *sleep*.

Do I sleepwalk? I don't think so, but, then again, I'd be the last person to know about it. It seems like a big leap to go from shuffling from room to room to meticulously arranging a crime scene, but is it really more of a leap than ghosts? I mean, come on.

I sigh, rinsing shampoo from my hair. The outlets in this place might be hit or miss, but the shower works great. The hot water scalds me red, and the pressure is killer. Just the way I like it. With how sweaty I was yesterday, I would've rather showered in scorpions than hot water, but today, the rising steam calms me. The rhythmic pounding of the water hitting my skin is soothing, too, scouring away my worries.

Dad pounds on the door. "Hurry it up in there!"

I groan. The joys of sharing a bathroom. "I'm coming, I'm coming," I grumble, turning off the faucet and reaching for a towel. I wrap myself in it and turn toward the mirror out of habit. Then I scream.

"What is it? Did you slip?" Dad calls from outside.

I rip the door open and gesture at the mirror with a shaking, dripping arm. My name is written in condensation on the glass, bleeding at the edges.

"We have to get out of here right now," I say, my voice rising to a shriek. "This place is haunted, and the ghosts know my name!"

"Ghosts again." Dad shakes his head, almost amused. "I should've guessed."

"Yes, ghosts!" I stamp my foot. "Real, live, dead, actual pervert ghosts! In the bathroom!" I tighten the towel around me. "Watching me *shower!*"

My dad frowns. The joke's getting old. "How am I supposed to know you didn't write that yourself?"

I snarl in frustration. "Even if I had enough time to write anything between when you knocked and I opened the door, why would I bother?"

Dad lists off reasons on his thick fingers. "To keep up this ghost charade of yours, to convince me to take you back to Texas, because you don't feel like I pay enough attention to you—"

"You don't," I cut in, "but that's not what this is about. I—"

"No, you listen to me," Dad snaps, and I fall silent. "I don't know if this is some kind of stupid cry for help—"

A bitter laugh bursts out. I remember all the nights I cried myself to sleep after Mom left, wishing he would come comfort me. Of course, he never did.

Then I think back to when I was twelve, in the closet literally and figuratively, with some stupid scarf of Maria Elena's wrapped around my neck so I could—what? Choke myself? I don't even know. I just wanted to die, but I couldn't even figure out how to do that right, so I was crying, and crying, and crying, and Dad should've been able to hear me through the wall, but he didn't care. Maybe that was as close as he could get to kindness, not coming in to yell at me to knock it off.

"Believe me, Dad, you'd be the last person I'd cry to."

For an instant, he almost looks hurt. Then he looks like he wants to hurt me. His voice comes out cold and cruel. "Who else would you cry to? Your mommy?"

I go rigid. All I want is to get as far away from him as possible, but I can't move. Even if I could, he's blocking the doorway. The ghosts, the house, my dad, my mom—I don't want to deal with it. Any of it. I feel trapped. Buried alive, like in my dream.

Tears trickle down my cheeks, startling me out of freeze mode.

"She loves me," I say, because it's the easiest, truest thing I can.

"She abandoned you," Dad retorts. "She left us—all of us. You hold everything I do against me so you can play the victim, but at least I *stayed*. But go ahead and worship that little picture of yours. Make a shrine to the parent who left instead of the one who actually bothered to raise you."

"It's not a shrine!" My voice breaks. And it's not. Shrines are for the dead, and I know my mother's alive. "She'll come back for me."

"Sure she will." Dad's words drip with lethal sarcasm. "It's only been six years."

"Shut up!" I cry.

Dad advances, raising an open hand. "Don't you tell me to shut up!" I flinch, and something like regret passes over my father's face.

"She'll come back," I repeat, crying so hard my teeth start chattering. "She has to come back…"

Dad runs a hand through his gray-streaked hair. "Enough," he says gruffly. "We're not talking about your mom anymore, and we're damn sure not talking about ghosts." He leaves without another word.

Cold and vulnerable beneath the towel, I shiver. The letters of my name are dripping in long streaks, melting toward the bottom of the mirror. Numbly, I press a finger to the glass, then draw a straight line down. I draw another, then another, then I swipe through the misty *Francisca* with my fingers spread, leaving a shiny, jagged void in the middle of the steamy mirror.

I change, then go to my room and sit on my bed, on top of the blanket. The bed's still unmade from this morning, but I don't care. The window is closed. Will it be open when I wake up? I don't care about that either. I guess it's hard to get worked up about the afterlife when my own life hardly feels worth living.

I'm alone. Truly, utterly alone. My mom is who knows where, my friends and Tia Lola are a thousand miles away, and my dad's just on the other side of the hall, but I feel further from him than anyone.

But I don't care about him. I don't care about anything. I don't care if this cursed house gives me the worst nightmare I've ever had—I'm going to sleep, ending this worthless day.

I should know better than to tempt fate like that.

Chapter Five

"It's not stealing if it grows on trees," Maria Elena explains, leaning halfway over the Gonzalez's stone wall to pluck one of their pomegranates.

That's how I know I'm dreaming—my goody-two-shoes sister would never. She looks like she did in the last dream, and so do I, with the braided hair and a sunflower behind my ear.

My stomach grumbles—I'm nervous about being caught, but Maria Elena hears and mistakes it for hunger. She smiles at me, tossing the pomegranate up and down, catching it smoothly in the palm of her hand.

"Don't worry," she tells me, "I'll share, just like our oranges."

Now I'm hungry. My mouth waters. The oranges that grow on our tree are the sweetest in the whole village. I can almost, but not quite, reach them from my bedroom window. I never pick them myself, though. I leave that to Maria Elena, who can shimmy up to the highest branches like she was born for it. If I ever tried, I would be trembling the whole time, worried the branches would give way, but Maria Elena has always been brave.

I wonder if it always works that way, with sisters—one of them gets what the other one lacks, and, together, they fit perfectly.

I think about my best friends, Abril and Maya San Miguel. Even though they're identical twins, there's no mistaking one for the other, once you know what to look for. Maya laughs louder, smiles wider, and is always quicker to start up a game or crack a joke. Maya likes to make things happen while Abril would rather wait and see. Sometimes I wonder if *we* were supposed to be twins, and Maya and

Maria Elena should have been sisters.

Then I'm in my room, watching the orange tree through the open window. Golden light slants through gaps in its vibrant leaves. Maria Elena is walking a branch like a tightrope, and Maya is giggling down below, with Abril standing some distance away. Maria Elena reaches upward—

Her skin rots black, then drips from the bone like candle wax.

My mouth is open in horror, but I can't make a sound. I just watch, helpless, as her skin melts away, leaving the skeleton behind. At first, it's only the neck down. The skin falls off so slowly, so heavily. I hear it pattering thickly against the dirt. I hear Maya coughing and choking down below, but I can't look at anything but Maria Elena, who's smiling as her skin decomposes, until I'm gazing at a grinning skull with oranges in its eye sockets. The skeleton collapses, and there's nothing but the tree.

Then I'm in the tree. Not in its branches—*inside*. Trapped in the trunk. I struggle, but rough bark clenches around me, scraping my skin raw. My blood is sluggish, as if it has been replaced with sap. I can't breathe, let alone cry out in agony as my bones begin to lengthen, then splinter.

Crack. Crack.

They're becoming branches.

My legs are dragged downward, into the earth. I'm being pulled in both directions. Any second now, I'll be torn apart.

Panic overrides the physical torture. Somehow, I know I've brought this upon myself.

I can't cry out, but I feel the words: *No! Stop! This isn't what I wanted! I'm not supposed to be here! I belong—*

But I can't remember.

A hundred years of days and nights glance across my bark. Just when I've convinced myself this is forever, I finally wake up.

The first thing I do is scream, but it's such a relief to have working lungs, I can't help but laugh. A trembling giggle gives way to hysterical hyena cackling. Soon, I'm crying, gasping for breath, rocking back and forth in bed, arms around my knees. The soft undersides of my arms press against my bare legs, which are sticky with sweat, prickly with hair. Skin, skin, skin! I am never complaining about acne again.

Bit by bit, the giddiness bleeds out. Even though I just woke up, I'm spent. I fall back onto the bed, gazing at the ceiling. Cold air whistles past me, and I sigh. I don't need to look at the window to know that it's open.

This should bother me more than it does. So should the fact that my phone is still dead, and, thanks to my fight with Dad last night, I can't just go up to him and remind him about my charger. There's no chance he'll buy one for me now. I could walk into town and get one myself, but the idea of running away has lost its urgency.

Leaving this house won't bring Mom back.

That shouldn't be the only thing that matters. It should be enough that Tia Lola loves me, and I have my friends, and hobbies, and whatever. And it's not like I've got nothing to look forward to—I want to go to college, get a car of my own, see what the next Luna Del Sol album is about. Life's not so bad when I look at the little things. Together, they should add up to something.

But Mom missing—it's not just a big thing, it's *everything*. It's a hole inside me that all good things fall into.

I'm not crying, but tears from earlier are growing hard on my face. My cheeks itch, but I make no move to scratch them. I just stare upward at nothing. Outside, the sun gets brighter and brighter, until I'm shielding my eyes. It's almost enough to make me get up and grab my sunglasses. Instead, I turn over on my side and pull the blanket over my head.

I lie there for however long, not sleeping, but not all that awake, either. Drifting. Then Dad knocks on my door hard enough to rattle the frame.

"You better not still be asleep in there!" he bellows.

I groan, shucking off the blanket. "I'm awake."

"It's already ten o'clock. If I ever tried to sleep in late like this, my father would've—"

So I get out of bed. I get dressed. I even make breakfast for me and Dad—plain scrambled eggs for me, eggs and chorizo for him. The spicy smell of sausage makes me sick, so I pick at my food. I don't even really like eggs—they're just the only thing Dad taught me how to cook. He thinks a man knowing how to make anything else would be *gay*. Don't ask me what's so straight about eggs. I couldn't tell you.

Now that I'm up and about, the idea of walking to town to buy a charger has a little more appeal. Is life worth living? Maybe not, but I don't know if I want to wait around and see if death-by-ghost is any better.

Unfortunately, I don't think Dad will give me permission to leave the house. It's safer not to ask. He's already mad at me for sleeping in, mad about last night, mad he got a chunk of eggshell in his breakfast, mad that the TV in the living room keeps cutting to static while he tries to watch the sports channel.

Actually, everything electric in the house seems to be acting up. When I snuck into his office so I could use the computer to IM my friends, it wouldn't turn on, like my phone the day before. Good thing I hightailed it out of there before Dad could catch me, otherwise he'd accuse me of breaking it.

Lights keep flickering, and the bulb in the upstairs hall went out. There's a little pool of light at the top of the stairs, then a long stretch of darkness between Dad's room and mine. The hall has no windows. My room is blindingly bright by comparison, but orange tree branches cast strange shadows. They look like grasping hands.

I turn on the light to try and make them go away, switching on my desk lamp, too, for good measure, but it doesn't help. Then the light from the lamp gets brighter and brighter, and I hear it buzzing, and there's nothing to do but turn it off before it explodes. Just to be safe, I pull the plug, wind the cord around the lamp, and shove it in a desk drawer. Later, the drawer is wedged shut. Even pulling with all my weight, I can't get it open. Whatever. I don't need the lamp anyway. When the overhead light sputters out, leaving me in semi-darkness as the sun sets, I take it as my sign to turn in for the day.

Will I have another nightmare? Probably. Is the ghost the reason the lights are acting up, the reason my desk won't open? Probably. I don't know. Maybe there's only room for one big mystery in life, and I already have mine.

I used to get like this back at home, too, sometimes, sans ghost. Tia Lola says spending so much time in bed, losing interest in things I care about, is a sign of depression. She thought it might help to see a counselor. Fat chance of that, me going to some white lady's office so she can call me by my deadname and tell me I'm sick in the head. That stuff costs money, too, and no way would my dad be willing to pay. Therapy is even gayer than a man who can cook.

Plus, what's counseling supposed to do? I don't need a stranger to tell me why I'm sad. Believe me, I know.

Dad yells at me to take a shower, so I do. I keep it quick and cold so there won't be any steam, that way the ghost can't draw on the mirror again. As I'm toweling off, I hear a crash, but it's distant enough that I decide I don't care. Dad brushes past me in the dark hall, heading for his room in a hurry. I wonder what's got him so riled up. I pass his office, then reach for my door, which opens before I can even turn the knob.

The sun disappeared completely while I was in the shower. My whole room is in shadow. I can barely make out the dim shapes of my bed, desk, and dresser. It seems darker than it should be, but it's probably the orange tree's fault. Those branches could be blocking out what little light is left.

I go to put my clothes in the hamper, but a cold, sudden pain shoots up my foot.

I cry out. The foot throbs. Now it feels hot, gushing. I lift it hastily and hop toward the dresser on one leg, leaning against it for support. I touch my foot with trembling fingers. My hand comes away sticky with blood.

Chapter Six

lood. Something about blood makes me stupid. The sight of it just shuts me down. Now, even though I can't see it, just knowing it's there—that I have a wound *oozing*—makes my thoughts slow to a crawl.

I'm standing there almost in a trance when my dad's dim shape fills the doorway.

"What are you screaming about this time?" he asks with a slur.

I push out one breath, then another. I don't want my voice to shake when I answer him. The last thing I need is to be punished for weakness on top of everything else.

"I cut my foot." There—I don't sound scared, just numb.

Dad nods loosely. "That sucks."

"What if I need stitches?" I ask, unable to keep a note of panic at bay. Stitches are even worse than blood, in my book. The thought of having my skin all stitched up like Frankenstein grosses me out.

"It can't be that deep," Dad dismisses.

Like he would know! He hasn't even seen the cut yet, but that's my dad for you.

I try to imagine what it's like to have the kind of dad that worries when their kid hurts themselves instead of the kind that just insists they soldier through. I still have a scar on my calf from the time I burned myself tripping over a campfire when I was seven and my dad's solution was to stick some bandaids on it. Believe it or not, slapping adhesives on a burn wasn't the best idea, and when the doctor insisted I take them off, a bunch of skin peeled off with them. Another success for Dr. Diego Fuentes. Not.

Still, after the past few days, if my dad *did* suddenly care about me and insist on taking me to the hospital, I'd probably think he was possessed by a vengeful spirit and that he was taking me off to sacrifice me or something. At least his usual brand of A-plus parenting is familiar, and annoyance is helping me get past the shock of the blood.

"What did you cut it on, anyway?" Dad asks.

"I don't know."

Dad huffs. "Well, first of all, let's turn on the light—" It switches on for him no problem. Maybe he is in league with the ghosts after all. "That's your problem—glass," he announces, nodding like he's proud of himself for cracking the case. "There's broken glass all over the floor. Did you drop a picture frame or somethi—"

"No, no, no!" I cry, dropping to my knees.

With shaking, blood-slicked hands, I push glittering shards of glass out of the way, clearing them away from the picture they once framed: my mom smiling at her wedding. Tears well in my eyes as I lift the photo, and I hear my dad make a grunt of disgust low in his throat. I turn on him.

"*You* did this! You're still mad about yesterday—you called it a shrine—you didn't want me to have this—you—you—" I'm panting with rage. I can't speak.

I know it didn't just fall. I had it all the way back against the wall, for one, and if it did fall, it would've fallen face down. I wouldn't have been able to see the picture right away. No, he did this. He picked it up and threw it. That was the crash I heard in the shower. That was why he was rushing past me in the hall.

"I haven't even *been* in your room," my dad says.

It could have been the ghosts, a small voice in my head suggests, but I tell that voice to shut up.

This is just like my dad. Didn't he smash my dollhouse? Didn't he throw his phone and shatter the windshield when I made a wrong turn during driving practice? Didn't he threaten to break my violin in half more times than I could count? He wants to punish me, to make sure I know there's not one thing I love that he can't take from me, nothing he can't destroy.

"You ruin everything!" I cry. "It's all your fault! It's your fault my picture's broken, your fault we're stuck here, your fault I don't have a mom!"

Dad takes a heavy step forward. "Your mom made her choice. She left."

A horrible, mocking smile twists my face. "Do you really think I don't know why? The walls back home were pretty thin, you know. I could *hear* what you were doing to her." Then my face collapses, and I'm sobbing.

I remember those horrible nights listening to my parents scream, torn between wanting to run away and wanting to do something—anything—to make it stop. In the end, I just lay in bed, paralyzed, staring up at the ceiling and wishing it was morning already. Mom would smile at me beneath her thick makeup as she made breakfast, Maria Elena would hum as she set the table, and we could all pretend everything was fine.

I hate my dad for what he did to my mom, and I hate myself for doing nothing to stop it. What was a little kid supposed to do? I don't know, but I can't shake the feeling that I might have made a difference if I only tried. Now I'll never know.

Maybe Mom would have stuck around if I had defended her.

Maybe, if I proved myself worthy, she would have taken me with her.

Maybe being stuck with Dad is what I deserve for being such a coward.

No. I'm older now. I'm not some helpless kid. One way or another, I am getting out of this house.

I hobble forward, my injured foot trailing blood, and try to leave the room. Dad grabs my wrist.

"Where do you think you're going?"

The obvious answer is back to San Antonio. As for how I'm getting there—I haven't thought that far ahead. I've got no money, no working phone, and one functioning foot. Doesn't matter. I'll hitchhike, carjack, or crawl my way there—whatever it takes.

I yank as hard as I can, but I can't pull my arm out of my dad's grasp. His hand is hot and rough around my wrist, thick fingers digging into my flesh. When he finally lets go, he'll probably leave behind a bracelet of bruises just like the ones I used to see on Mom. They were the only jewelry Dad ever gave her besides a wedding ring.

"Just let me go!" I yell, pulling harder. When that doesn't work, I plant both feet firmly on the ground, crying out in pain, and wrench myself away with all my weight.

Before I can even try to run, Dad seizes me by the shoulders. His breath is hazy with beer, and his eyes are horrible—black coals and red fire, a dead thing smoldering.

I've made a terrible mistake.

"Please, let go," I whisper, cringing at how broken my voice sounds.

He slaps me, and it stings, and I should hate him for doing it, and I'm sure I do, but not as much as I hate myself for ever thinking I could escape it.

Because I really do try, you know? I keep out of his space. I answer to my deadname. I pay attention to his moods and know better than to ask him for anything when he's angry. But I'm not always good at it, and I lose my temper, so I guess I have no one but myself to blame.

It must be my fault, right, if he treats me like this and not perfect Maria Elena?

If it's all because of something I've done, that implies there's something *else* I can do to make it stop. But, so far, after all these years, I haven't found it.

"Disrespect me like that again and see what happens," Dad snarls.

When he adds that I've lost computer privileges for a month, I'm too numb to care. Does he really think there's any punishment worse than just having him as a father?

He leaves the room, and I stand there for a while. All the broken glass winks up at me. My mother's frozen face smiles. Then the light above me flickers and goes out, and I hear the orange tree rap against the window to my back. Eventually, I limp out of the room, not because I care what the ghost has up its sleeve, but because my foot is still bleeding and I should probably try to make that stop unless I want to die from the most pathetic wound of all time.

We have a first aid kit in the kitchen, but no way am I going downstairs. Instead, I grit my teeth and make it to the bathroom, where I rinse my foot in the tub. The rushing water stings, but I grit my teeth and stay there until it comes away clear rather than pink. Then I towel off and wrap my foot in toilet paper.

It still hurts, and I'm leaning against the wall on the way back to the bedroom, but there's no blood. I don't see why it matters now, blood or no blood, but a small, stubborn part of me insists that this is a good thing. No blood is good. Staying alive is good.

When I return to my room, the light is working again. A sharp glittering below catches my eyes, and the part of me that's capable of caring directs my eyes down.

The glass has rearranged itself into concentric circles, jagged edges pointing toward a picture in the middle. It's not the wedding picture. It's the one I spilled red nail polish on the day we moved in, and my mother has shards of glass driven through her eyes.

My first thought is that maybe my dad didn't break the wedding picture after all.

My second thought is that I want this ghost *dead*.

I know that doesn't make sense. I don't care. I want to find out exactly who this ghost is so I can bring them back to life so I can kill them again. Painfully. All the anger and disappointment I felt toward myself after my dad hit me suddenly has a new direction: the ghost that set me up.

Where does this *thing* get off, ruining my life?

One thing's for certain—running away is out of the question now. I'm staying right here until I get some answers.

Chapter Seven

You'd think after a night like that, I'd be in for some pretty gruesome nightmares, but I don't dream at all. I do wake up in the middle of the night, though.

The first time it happens, I catch myself reaching for the bedroom door. Sleepwalking. Great. Is the stress of the haunting getting to me, or is the ghost puppeteering my body? Neither option is good, but what can I do? I throw myself back into bed and turn over on my side, facing the wall.

Darkness. Then I'm standing at the top of the stairs.

My heart races as I look down at the steep drop. Is the ghost going to throw me down and snap my neck? I suck in a deep breath. If the ghost wanted me dead, it probably would've just killed me by now. But what is its goal, then? Is it trying to lead me somewhere?

Doesn't matter. I'm not going.

I return to the bedroom, locking the door this time, and fall asleep the instant I hit the mattress.

Crea-ea-eak.

The sound of a door opening jolts me awake. My hand is wrapped around something cold and slick, but I pull back as if burned. I remember locking the bedroom door before falling asleep. For a moment, I'm convinced that's where I am—the bedroom.

The door's open just a crack, but I can tell it doesn't lead into the hallway. The darkness beyond is too deep.

Where am I?

Cold seizes my body. I'm shivering too hard to control my hands. As badly as I want to, I can't let go of the doorknob. I continue to pull it open, slowly, slowly, until I see the shadowy staircase that leads to the basement. I haven't been down there yet. My skin prickles in the chilling, rotting air, and I know I don't want to. There's something down there, or a passage some*where*, and the ghost is dragging me toward it.

Down in the distance, I hear voices echoing, but no words. I can just catch cadences: a man rumbling, a woman raving, a girl crying—and a whimper.

My legs are trembling from the effort of holding still. I feel a presence telling me to move. Am I possessed? I'm not sure. It doesn't feel like the ghost is inside me, taking control. It feels more like my dad when he's drunk, pushing and pulling me wherever he wants me to go. Hands on my back are shoving me forward, but I stand my ground as the voices below get louder.

The woman screams, but not like before—a horrible shriek, like she's been shot or stabbed. She cries out, and this time, I can hear exactly what she's saying:

"Francisca, help me!"

The voice is mother's.

I throw the door open with so much force, it bangs against the wall, then rebounds, slamming me in the back. I crumble. My knees hit the first stair, and my palms scrape against the second. A splinter pierces my right hand. That sharp little gasp of pain clears my head a bit, just enough for me to realize I'm being tricked.

"No," I whisper behind gritted teeth, slowly forcing myself upright and turning from my mother's screams. I won't let this ghost use my mom to manipulate me. I close the door, lock it, and climb to the second floor.

I fumble in the dark for my backpack. Feeling my way around the room, I make it to my desk and grab my dead phone and charger. I toss them into the backpack. I feel the slick lenses of my sunglasses, which I slide into the front pocket. With my wallet already there, there's just enough room. I zip it shut. I grope around in my dresser until my hands come across something that feels like a t-shirt and a rougher something that's probably denim shorts. I change as quickly as I can, sling the backpack over my shoulder, and run.

I don't know where I'm going. *Away* is enough.

Down the stairs, out the door, into the night. I run until the sound of rustling branches fades behind me and all I hear are my own thudding footsteps. The foot I cut last night throbs with each impact, and I still haven't pulled the splinter in my right hand. My lungs ache, choking on each dusty breath, but I force myself to keep moving until the dirt road gives way to a proper street. There, at the fork in the road, I bend over, hands on my knees, and catch my breath.

I haven't run like that in years. The first thing to come to mind is when they had us run the mile back in middle school, only God knows I never tried that hard. I've been able to get a waiver out of P.E. the past couple years since I play on the school's bowling team. I've got killer arms but zero cardio.

Thinking about school and my old, normal life—even if it's a gazillion miles away—helps me calm down. The sun is rising and, as I take breath after breath, I imagine my way through my friends' mornings: Cat applying strawberry lip gloss and texting her boy-friend of the month, Angie dripping sugar water into her ant farm and jotting down observations in her sticker-covered notebook. Tia Lola is probably still lounging in bed with her hair in curlers while Dolores makes breakfast. And here I am in the middle of nowhere, running from ghosts.

What now?

I slowly straighten up. Now, I get rid of it. It seems like it'd be easier to figure out how if I knew who was haunting me and why. In movies, houses are usually haunted after someone dies in them—like Dad's great uncle or whoever he was, the one he inherited the house from.

I growl at myself in frustration. It sure would be nice if I could remember his name. What was it? Paco, right? Well, I know he was a Fuentes, and he died not too long ago. That should be enough in-formation to track down an obituary. It's not much to go on, but at least it's something to look for, and I have a pretty good idea where I can find it.

As the sun creeps upward, I make my way to the library I saw the other day.

The squat, one-story library's in what you might call the heart of the town, except that makes it sound warm and welcoming, and central Claudesville is absolutely none of those things. Most of the buildings, like city hall and the post office, are just as bad off as the new house. A few, like a long-abandoned train station, are even worse.

Next to the library, there's a stone cathedral surrounded by a graveyard full of crumbling, tilted headstones. I wonder if the ghost haunting me was buried there. I shudder. If I don't find anything at the library, that might be a good place to look for clues, but I'm not poking around the graveyard unless it's absolutely necessary.

The library's whitewashed walls gleam in the early morning light. It looks angelic. Or ghostly. And definitely closed. I know that before I even try to open the glass front doors. The sign says it opens at eight, and, if I had to guess, it's probably closer to six right now. There's nothing to do but wait.

I drift around, looking for a bench to nap on, but I get distracted by the big cement square I noticed from across the street. Up close, I can see the top of it—there's a jagged pit in the middle, like something's been torn off. I walk around it and spot a bronze placard, covered in dust and speckled with patina. It only has two words engraved on it: *Nuestra Claudia.*

I find a bench and curl up, wrapped protectively around my backpack in case anyone tries to steal it. I wake up to a piping, unfamiliar voice calling, "Hello? Hello?" Then, in a whisper: "Agosta, do you think she's dead?"

"Not dead," I announce, uncurling and sitting up. The sun is fully up now, and I squint into the light, fumbling for my sunglasses with one hand. Once they're on and I can see clearer, I see two identical women watching me with concern. They're both compact, dark-haired, and wearing white blouses. The one on the left has glasses and a gray skirt, and the one on the right is in khakis.

"Oh, good," says Glasses.

Khakis nods. "We haven't had anyone die on library grounds yet."

I can't help but notice the *yet.* I clutch my backpack a bit tighter.

"Most of our patrons are getting up in years these days," Glasses explains.

I don't loosen my grip. "Are you two librarians?"

"Of course!" they exclaim in unison.

Khakis clasps her hands, eyes gleaming with hope. "Please tell us you're here for a book. We'll help you find anything you're looking for."

"Even one of the bad ones they don't keep in schools," Glasses adds with a wink.

Khakis beams at me like I'm a long-lost friend. "We're just so glad to meet someone your age who's interested in reading."

"Especially during the summer."

"I'm Julia San Miguel, by the way," says Khakis in a rush, holding out her hand to shake. I take it gingerly. It's starting to get hot out, and I'm already sweating. "And this is my twin, Agosta."

Julia and Agosta San Miguel. There's something familiar about those names, but I can't quite place them. I know I haven't met them before—I'd definitely remember this pair of wackos.

At least they seem friendly and willing to answer questions. I'm pretty sure the librarian at my old school put me on some kind of hit list after I lost that stupid copy of *Macbeth* I had to borrow for class. Saying the name of the play is supposed to be bad luck—how about losing a copy of it? Maybe that librarian died, and he's the one after me now, trying to track down that lost book.

"I'm looking for obituaries, actually," I tell the librarians. "Do you keep those kinds of records here, or old newspapers, or something?"

"Yes, of course!" Julia exclaims. "The archives! Yes, you can find those down in the basement, all the way back to 1812, when the town was founded."

"It was called Nuestra Claudia then," Agosta chimes in.

I glance at the torn-up statue. "Was it named after someone?"

"Yes, but the gringos who took over either didn't know or didn't care," says Julia, reaching up to straighten the pencil tucked behind her right ear. "When they changed the name, they masculinized *and* anglicized it."

"In 1848."

"Yes, 1848—the year the Mexican-American War ended."

Agosta looks wistful. "This place really has a fascinating history."

Julia's smile sags. "Few people remember that anymore."

"And those that do are dying out," said Agosta somberly. "Soon, it will all be forgotten."

"Um, the obituaries?" I remind them.

"Oh, right! Yes, yes, yes," says Julia with an embarrassed little laugh. She turns to her sister, who is halfway to the door. "Agosta—"

Agosta pauses "What?"

"Do you want to take her down there, or should I?"

"I'll do it," Agosta replies with a grin. She turns to me with a confidential air. "Julia there is scared of the basement. She can't deal with the spiders."

I make a face. I don't like spiders, either, but they beat ghosts. Resigned, I fall into step behind Julia.

Agosta opens the door with a flourish, and I step inside. The air is a little cooler here, but not by much. A lone fan twirls on the high ceiling, moving so slowly I can make out each individual blade. Dust and dead flies coat the nearest window sills. Just as I'm wondering when's the last time anyone's cleaned this dump, Julia scurries over to the front desk and rifles beneath it, pulling out a black feather duster.

"My sister and I are the only ones who work here," she explains, dusting off a nearby shelf. "We keep everything in order ourselves."

"Everything" seems to mean five splintering bookshelves. If the archives go back to 1812, they must be way better stocked. At least, I hope they are. If I don't find what I'm looking for here, it's the graveyard, and, after that, I don't know where to go.

Agosta jangles her key ring until she finds what she's looking for—what looks like the smallest key of the bunch. She leads me to a doorway in the back and unlocks it, gesturing to the dimly lit staircase. My stomach lurches as I remember the night before, but I don't get any kind of malevolent feeling from this staircase, or from Julia and Agosta. Still, I hesitate.

"Right this way—" Agosta looks at me expectantly, and I realize she's waiting for my name.

"Francisca," I tell her, lifting my chin. "Francisca Luna Fuentes."

If she's surprised that someone who looks like me has such a feminine name, she doesn't show it. "Francisca," she repeats, still beaming. "Come with me."

She looks so eager, I half expect her to grab my arm and drag me along, and I'm grateful that she doesn't. Being touched, especially by strangers, always puts me on edge. I think I can trust her, though. She used my name.

Agosta leads me downstairs to a dank, poorly lit basement. Somehow, it's even hotter down here than it is outside.

"The furnace is down here," Agosta explains before I can ask. "I've been banging away at it for months, but I just can't turn it off." She pants and tugs at the collar of her blouse, then slips her smile back into place. "You said you were looking for obituaries, right? Do you have a particular name or date in mind?"

"Kind of?" I say. "A relative of mine died recently—a Fuentes."

Agosta nods thoughtfully. "Fuentes, Fuentes…it's not ringing any bells. Do you know their first name?"

"No," I admit, a bit embarrassed. "I think it was Paco, but I'm not really sure. I never knew the guy."

"Genealogical research?" Agosta guesses.

"Kind of." No way am I telling this lady that I'm hunting ghosts.

"When did he pass away?"

Even though Dad and I just moved here, he found out about the house right at the start of summer, so the owner should've died around then. "May of this year."

"Those newspapers should be right over here," she says, directing my attention to a gray filing cabinet that's taller than I am. Identical ones line the basement from wall to wall. "Second drawer from the top. You take your time and search for whatever you need, and, if you have any questions, come upstairs and find me or Julia, okay?"

"Okay. Thanks."

Her footsteps fade away as I open the filing cabinet. It's full of issues of the local newspaper: *The Claudesville Caller*. I find the May issues pretty quickly and take them with me to a nearby table. I make sure to pick one that's as far away from the room's cobwebby corners as possible. I skip straight to the obituary section of each paper.

Before long, I find a Fuentes:

Pablo Flores-Fuentes, died May 11, 2010. Gone but not forgo
That's all it says.

I curl my hands into fists to keep from tearing the paper to shreds. That's it? All the other obituaries are at least two lines—so-and-so passed away in a bike accident, lives on in their three children, will always be remembered for their distinct fashion sense, etcetera. But not Paco. Pablo, I mean. I groan. He was so forgettable, they forgot to finish writing his obituary, and even now I can't remember his name. Is that why he's haunting me, because he's mad his life was so boring?

I slump in defeat. Within seconds, my forehead is sweated to the table. Gross, but whatever. There's no sense in getting unstuck—where would I even go? Back to the house? Yeah, right.

This whole idea was stupid. Who says Paco-Pablo is the ghost that's after me, anyway? The house has been around for more than a hundred years. I bet a ton of people have died in it, and I don't know anything about them—their names, their lives, the way they died.

Why they would try to drag me into the basement, smash my mother's wedding picture, behead dolls, or whisper at me from inside the tree.

Inside the tree.

I remember the most recent nightmare I had—the one where I became one with the tree. I grimace, remembering the skin-tearing, bone-cracking transformation, but I force myself to think past it. Before then, I was that girl with the braid and the sunflower, the one the grandfather called Girasol in the dream before. But that wasn't her real name.

It was Francisca.

Chapter Eight

Francisca Flores.

The name shivers over me, and I know I'm right.

I need to start keeping these names straight. I sling my backpack onto the table and dig through it, wishing I had thought to bring a notebook. All I can come up with are a red pen probably left over from last school year and a wadded-up gum wrapper. I uncrumple the wrapper, trying to smooth it out as best I can, and write "Francisca Flores" in the smallest letters possible. Under it, I add "Maria Elena Flores" and, after glancing at the obituary in the paper: "Pablo Flores-Fuentes."

I hesitate, thinking of the missing sculpture outside, and add "Claudia." If a bunch of gringos tore down my statue and renamed my town, I'd haunt houses, too. Right now, I'm not discounting anything. Any dead person's name I can think of is going on this list.

The next names that come to mind are Julia and Agosta. Since those two are obviously alive, I don't bother writing them down. But they do remind me of another pair of names: Abril and Maya San Miguel. Same last name—maybe the librarians are descended from those twins in my dream.

Does that matter? Maybe not, but if Julia and Agosta's family has lived here for such a long time, it might be easier to get information from them than these musty archives. I slip the gum wrapper into my pocket and fan myself with one hand. Plus, it won't hurt to get a break from the furnace. I put the newspaper with the obituary back in the cabinet and head upstairs.

Julia is sitting behind the front desk, watching the glass doors expectantly. Her face lights up when she sees me.

"Hello again. Did you find what you were looking for?"

"Not exactly. So…" I decide to start off as casually as I can. "Is your family from around here?"

"Oh, yes. We've been here since the very beginning," says Julia proudly. "You can find San Miguels in every generation since the town started keeping records, and there's stories about us from before even then!"

"But there won't be any in *your* generation until our no-good brother finally settles down!" Agosta calls from behind a bookshelf.

I want to ask about Abril and Maya, but I have no idea what I'll say if Julia asks me how I know those names. One hand in my pocket, I roll the balled up gum wrapper between two fingers, thinking about other names on the list.

"What about the Flores family? Are they a big deal? The relative I was looking up earlier was a Flores-Fuentes," I explain before they can ask. There—a perfectly logical explanation, one that doesn't involve weird ghost-dreams.

"Flores," Julia repeats, nodding. "Yes, that family has been around almost as long as the San Miguels. You don't see much of them anymore."

"Because they're cursed," Agosta chimes in.

My voice breaks. "Cursed?"

"Oh, yes," says Agosta with relish, rubbing her hands together. She's abandoned all pretense of straightening books. "There were some strange happenings a hundred years ago, and ever since then, the Flores house has been haunted. Julia, do you know the address?"

Julia shakes her head.

"Well, if you're interested in this town's history, you might check out the Flores house sometime," Agosta tells me, a gleam in her eyes. "It's in the old neighborhood down the dirt road. All the houses look a fair bit alike, but you'd know the Flores house if you saw it—it has a huge orange tree up front and a sunflower patch in the back."

All the air is driven from my lungs. Having the haunting acknowledged by someone else makes it feel that much more real. I remember the cold feeling that came over me as I opened the basement door, the sight of my name dripping down the mirror, the broken glass stabbing through my mother's eyes. Real, all of it. I guess, even while I was researching, there was a part of me still hoping none of it had happened.

It takes a while to find my voice. "I know that house. I live there."

"Well, don't mind Agosta," says Julia with a maternal tone, turning quickly to scowl at her sister. "She loves a good ghost story, that's all."

"The curse is just a rumor," Agosta confesses, "but there *was* a string of deaths in the family at the turn of the century. One after the other, everyone who lived in that house died, and not peacefully, either."

Unease prickles my skin, but something about this doesn't make sense. "If everyone in the family died, how come a Flores-Fuentes owned the house before my dad inherited it?" I ask. I guess neither of those names are uncommon, but it seems like one hell of a coincidence.

"There were two brothers back then," Julia explains. "Diego Flores, who owned the house, and his younger brother Manuel, who moved away. Manuel Flores got the house after his brother's death, and it's been passed down that line ever since."

Agosta claps her hands. "You and your dad must be his descendants—how exciting!"

Yeah, I'm thrilled. "But Diego and his side of the family—you said they all died? What happened?" Instinctively, I look at Agosta. She's clearly the more morbid of the two. If either of them knows the specifics of a bunch of deaths a hundred years back, it would probably be her.

Sure enough, Agosta tells me, "Diego was the last to die, but it was a long time coming. He'd been drinking himself to death ever since he killed his wife."

"*What?*" I exclaim. Was that what I was overhearing in the basement last night, before I thought I heard Mom? "Why?"

"No one knows," says Julia softly.

"He had two daughters, but they died, too, a few years apart. One of them was killed in some sort of accident, and the other one—"

"Are you sure you want to know?" Julia cuts in, watching me closely.

"Of course she wants to know! Knowledge is power!" Agosta exclaims, disgusted by her sister's reticence.

Julia frowns. "Yes, but there's some information you have to be careful about when sharing, especially with someone of a particular age—"

"She killed herself, didn't she," I say flatly. Their silence tells me I'm right.

I've seen this song and dance before—adults avoiding the issue like there's a teenager out there that hasn't thought of it. *Suicide.* God. Life sucks and people kill themselves—tell me something I don't know.

Still. I feel nauseous, and I don't think it's because I haven't eaten today. My hands ball into fists, and my eyes sting like I'm about to cry, but of course I don't. I don't even know what I'd be crying about. I don't want to die. I don't.

I don't think so.

Chapter Nine

Even though I've got the information I came for, I stay in the library for a few more hours. I don't feel like confronting the ghost just yet, and I'm sure Dad will have something to say about my little disappearing act. Might as well put off dealing with both for as long as I can.

Since I don't feel like boiling alive in the basement, I walk through the narrow aisles upstairs, pick a few books more or less at random, and camp out on an ugly foam green armchair near the back wall. There's an outlet nearby. I plug in my phone charger. Sure enough, the phone beeps right away. The charger works fine—it was the house all along. I figure I might as well wait for my phone to reach a hundred percent, so I crack open one of the books.

I skim through the first third of a boring memoir, open a vampire romance novel to a random page only to quickly close it, flushing, then pick up the last book in my pile. The vibrant cover caught my attention: it's a photo of an ofrenda decorated with roses, bread, oranges, and sugar skulls. It turns out the book is in Spanish. I can understand a word or phrase here and there, but mostly I ignore the text and check out the pictures instead.

We never do anything for Dia de los Muertos in my family. Dad doesn't celebrate anything but a good gambling win, and Mom's white. She always went all out for Halloween, though, planning her costumes months in advance and charging neighborhood kids a quarter to check out haunted house scares in our garage.

One year, Mom covered the walls in black wrapping paper and got one of my cousins to stand in a corner wearing a matching jumpsuit and facemask and leap out at people. I can still remember the tilt of her chin when some crying kid's mother demanded she give her son his quarter back.

The memories keep coming, but I blink hard, not wanting to get lost in them. I'm not about to cry in public. Okay, so maybe "public" in this case is a library that's completely deserted except for me and a couple of kooky twins, but still. It's the principle.

I pick up the Dia de los Muertos book with determination and turn the page. I've always found it interesting, the mythos around it. It's a cool vision of the afterlife. I used to find it comforting to think that there's a bridge of some kind between the Land of the Dead and the Land of the Living, and even once you're dead, you can cross over and check things out sometime—if people remember you, at least. Now, the thought that the lines between life and death can be crossed is anything but comforting.

Eventually, my phone is charged, and I decide to head out and get some lunch. I'm starving. My plan is to get something at Walmart, but I'm so hungry, I stop at a run-down gas station along the way and get a bag of Cheetos and some soda instead. There's a sad little playground across the street, so I sit on one of the benches over there and eat facing a swing set with one of its chains broken.

This park wouldn't have been here a hundred years ago, when everyone in the Flores family was dying or being killed. I wonder what would have been in its place. A slight wind picks up, and it almost sounds like rushing water. I close my eyes, and I picture that river I saw in a dream, the one Maria Elena skipped stones across. I can hear it churning, louder than before, and I feel sunflowers swaying around me, but when I open my eyes, I'm on a hot plastic bench, staring at dusty, weedy earth.

The librarians said the Flores house was haunted, but, in moments like this, the whole town seems full of ghosts, or like it is one itself.

That's a cheery thought. I suck Cheeto dust off my fingers and try to think of a good distraction. I remember that my phone's working again, and neither of my friends have heard from me since the move, so I decide a conversation with quick-talking, always joking Angie is just what I need to shake these moody cobwebs off my mind.

"Francisca!" Angie cries as soon as she picks up the phone. "What up, girlfriend? It's been a few days—I thought you were dead!"

I wince. That joke hits a little too close to home. "Nope. Very much alive."

"You wanna hear the latest drama between me and Miss Catarina Garcia?"

"Uh, *yeah*," I say, leaning back and getting ready for the dirt. This should be good.

Angie really only hangs out with Cat because Cat hangs out with me, and the two of them are usually in a fight. Angie always uses Cat's full name whenever she's done something to piss her off. It's like she thinks she's Cat's mom.

"Well, you know Emilio, right?" Angie begins. "Emilio Leon?"

I nod, even though she can't see me. "Bowling Alley Boy," I say.

Angie's been crushing on one of the cashiers for months now. He's in the year above us in school, and I don't think he's anything to act a fool over, but Angie put up with my excruciatingly one-sided crush on Lila from math class, so I know better than to tease her.

Besides, the bowling alley at our local mall was my favorite place to hang out, even during the off-season, so anything that kept her coming back was fine by me. I loved the smooth firmness of the bowling balls, the heft in my hands, the sensation of letting go and watching it glide down the lane in a perfect, assured line, the roaring crash of pins falling. Everything was glow-in-the-dark, so I didn't even have to wear my sunglasses the way I usually did at the other stores, which were way too brightly lit.

I don't think Angie loves the place like I did—she complained about how tacky it was all the time—but she's super competitive, and if I was practicing, you could bet she was going to practice, too. Cat mostly came because I was there, and it was a good place to meet boys. That, and the bowling alley had the only vending machine in the mall with strawberry soda, her favorite.

"Well, Miss Catarina Garcia and I have been seeing him around the mall lately, and can you *guess* what she did? No, really—guess!"

I can't help but grin at Angie's indignant tone. "I'm sure whatever I say will pale in comparison before whatever horror of horrors she's unleashed."

Angie lowers her voice. "She *talked* to him! Can you *believe* it?"

"Cat? Talking to a boy?" I deadpan. "No way."

I hear a thump on Angie's end; I assume she's stamping her foot. "She knows how much I like him!"

"Everyone knows how much you like him," I interject.

Angie huffs, put out that I'm not taking her plight seriously. "That doesn't give Cat an excuse."

I laugh. If Angie's calling her Cat again, she must already be getting over it. "I hate to break it to you, Ange, but you're just as bad. Remember that field trip in eighth grade? If that drama between you got any worse, I would've put myself in witness protection."

"Maybe I should go into witness protection. I could use a new life, since there's clearly nothing left for me here," Cat sighs. "I'll dye my hair blonde, start over... I bet I'd look good blonde, actually! What do you think? Start junior year with a—oh." She's quiet for a moment. "I guess it's just hitting me that you're not gonna be there. Weird."

I'm not going to be there.

Angie and Cat are gonna fight and make up, and fight and make up, and fight and make up, and I'm not going to be there. Bowling season is going to start, and I'm not going to be there. Some new kid is going to join Spoken Word Club, too shy to jump on tables, and I'm not going to be there. I'm going to miss missing the prom, blowing it off to watch campy alien movies at Angie's house while receiving an endless string of text updates from Cat about spiked punch and who's making out with who.

My whole life is back at home, and I'm not going to be there.

Instead, I'm here, staring at a broken swing set and feeling a thousand years old. I wonder if this is how the ghost feels, watching life go on from a distance, jealous and alone.

Ghosts again. So much for a distraction.

"Listen, I'll talk to you later," I sigh, out of energy for the conversation. "Say hi to Cat for me."

Angie snorts. "Good one, Francisca. You'll be telling me to say hi to Student Council Rosa next." Student Council Rosa, not to be confused with History Rosa, who's fine, acted like she was everyone's best friend so they'd elect her student body president and then started acting like she was better than everyone the moment she won. Angie giggles in an imitation of Rosa during election season. "TTYL!"

This is where I'm supposed to put on a fake-perky voice, mimicking her tone, and go "XOX, BFF! Gooo, team!" but I'm too drained to fake it. I just say goodbye. Then I snap my phone shut and slump forward, head in my hands. Can't I make it through one conversation without being miserable? What's wrong with me?

No. No crying in public, and, yes, an empty playground still counts. Some kid and their mom might come around any moment. And that's what gets me—imagining some random kid holding their mother's hand, wishing my mom was around to hold mine. Stupid, stupid, *stupid*.

So, yeah, I cry for a while, marinating in self-pity like a chicken breast of despair, but I force myself to pull it together pretty fast. I put my phone away, hike up my backpack, and head back to the house full of ghosts where my dad is probably waiting to turn me into one for leaving without letting him know where I was going.

Dad doesn't look thrilled to see me, but he doesn't look angry either. He seems sober in more ways than one. There are dark shadows under his eyes, but they aren't red and unfocused like last night. They fix on me steadily, and I have to fight the urge to look away. A long silence stretches between us. It's unnerving.

"I'm sorry I left the house without asking," I say finally, guessing that he was trying to force a confession out of me.

"You can't just wander off in a strange place without telling me." His voice is gruff, but the words are distant, like he's saying one thing and thinking another. But he doesn't say anything else, and neither do I. After what feels like forever, I walk around him and go upstairs. I feel his eyes on my back every step of the way.

Something strange must have happened to make him act this way. Did my dad finally have an encounter with the ghost, too? Is that why he's acting weird around me, because he's embarrassed that he didn't believe me and doesn't want to admit it? Or maybe he's sorry he hit me. First time for everything, I guess.

For once, though, Dad is the least of my problems. Once I'm in my room, I close the door tight, pull the gum wrapper with the names in red out of my pocket, and take a deep breath. The orange tree outside the window is deathly still.

"Abril San Miguel," I say.

Nothing happens.

"Maya San Miguel."

Still nothing.

"Claudia. Pablo Flores-Fuentes. Maria Elena Flores."

I think I hear the slightest rustling in the orange tree outside, but I could be making it up.

I hesitate before reading the last name, though I don't even know what I expect to happen. I just have this sense that calling on the ghost—if this *is* the ghost—is crossing a line. Saying her name makes it that much more real. It's an invitation of sorts, a bridge from her world into mine. I think back to that Dia de los Muertos book—remembering the dead is what allows them to cross over. I don't know if I want to give her that. Will it make her more powerful? More dangerous? Do I even have a choice?

The bridge has already been crossed. The ghost is here. All I can do now is try to figure out what she wants and do what I can to send her away.

I take a deep breath. "Francisca Flores."

The wind howls in frenzied excitement. Orange tree branches batter the window, scraping the glass. The scent of citrus floods the room. I hear girls laughing, followed by a snap and a scream. I have a vision of myself waist-deep in sunflowers as distant figures walk calmly into a dark river without once turning back.

"Francisca," I say again, faintly. Then, because I have no idea what to say next: "Hey. Cool name."

The leaves rustle outside, and it almost sounds like laughter. I decide to take this as a good sign. Maybe if I build a rapport with the ghost, it'll be easier to convince her to leave me alone.

"Francisca," I repeat. "It's classic, you know? I picked it because of the Luna del Sol song. It's my favorite. Also, I thought it'd be funny to be a trans girl with 'cis' in my name." It occurs to me that someone who died in 1910 probably has no idea what I'm talking about. "Forget it. I guess what I'm trying to say is, uh, I get it. You. I get you, Francisca."

The wind goes quiet, like the ghost is listening to what I have to say.

I wrap my arms around myself, not because I'm cold, but because I'm trying to hold myself together. "I heard you killed yourself."

I gag suddenly. Something rough scratches my neck, pressing against my throat. Then the roughness spreads over my entire body, and I'm being pulled toward the sky and dragged underground at the same time. Then the horrible searing feeling fades, and I can breathe again.

"It was the tree," I whisper, rubbing my neck. "You hung yourself from the tree, and you're still there after all this time. Is that right?"

Wailing wind and scraping glass—nothing I can make sense of.

"You can control the tree, right? And the wind?" I guess. "Tap the window once for yes, and keep doing what you're doing if I'm wrong."

Silence. Then—a single tap.

I can't help it. I shudder.

"Listen," I say as strongly as I can, "you've done some messed up things around here. I'd probably do the same if I was dead and some rando moved into my house. But it has to stop. I bet you don't want to be stuck here anymore than I want to be haunted. I'm willing to do what I can to help you—I don't know. Cross over?"

She taps once, then over, and over, and over.

Yes, yes, yes, yes, yes.

"So, we want the same thing. That's good," I tell her. "We can be—" not friends. *Definitely* not friends. That is way too creepy. "We're on the same side," I say at last. "Can we agree on that?"

One tap.

I let out a shaky breath. "Okay, great. Now we just need to figure out how to get you out of here."

Easier said than done. I don't think there's any amount of tree-tapping that can communicate something like that, and that's assuming the ghost herself even knows what to do. She's probably just as lost as I am.

There's a soft but insistent scraping at the window. I move closer, and there's a slender branch prodding at the windowpane.

"You want me to open the window?" I ask, my heart sinking.

The branch lifts just enough to tap the glass.

You'd have to be crazy to do something like that.

"I'm crazy, I'm crazy, I'm crazy," I mutter, unlatching the window and lifting the glass.

The branch shoots into the room, growing rapidly. The yellowish leaves broaden, their color deepening to a rich jade. The branch fans out over my bed, creating a leafy canopy. White flowers blossom to life along the length of the branch, brightening the air with their delicate scent.

Then a single orange starts to swell right at the level of my eyes. At first, it's the size of a marble, then a clementine, then a fist. It's the most vivid orange I've ever seen, and it emits a strong yet sweet perfume. My mouth waters at the thought of the tender juiciness inside.

I reach for it in a daze, pulled toward it irresistibly, then yank my hand back in the instant before my fingers touch the glistening peel.

"Oh, no." I laugh harshly, turning away. "No, no, no. You must think I'm pretty stupid if you expect me to eat fruit off this death tree."

And I do feel stupid. What was I thinking, letting myself trust this ghost for even a second, after everything it's done? There's still a shard of glass on the floor, even though I swept up most of it, and anger rises in my chest as I watch it glitter.

This thing cut me. The ghost did that to me. It ruined my most prized possession. It spied on me through sunflowers, infested my dreams, tried to drag me into the screaming basement. For all I know, that basement is a portal to the Land of the Dead, and the ghost is trying to get me to take its place. What if *that* is what it means by crossing over—seizing my life and forcing me into its awful purgatory in the orange tree? Is that what will happen if I take a bite of that orange?

I don't know, but I'm not about to risk it.

Even though I've turned away, I can sense the orange behind me, pulsating like an organ. It's dangerous, and so is the ghost. A hundred years ago, there was a girl here who killed herself, and I might be able to empathize with her, but who's to say that the best parts of her aren't already long gone, leaving only something rotted and twisted behind?

I've got to get rid of it. That's all I can think—I've got to get rid of this ghost—but before I can even start brainstorming how, my dad yells my deadname from downstairs. I run.

Chapter Ten

Dad's standing by the front door, dangling his car keys. "Let's go for a drive," he tells me. No explanation. No smile on his face, either, but he doesn't look mad. He's got the same seriousness in his eyes that I saw earlier. I just hope to God he's not about to give me "the talk." I'd rather deal with the ghost. Still, it's not like I have a choice. I grab my sunglasses from upstairs and come back down, following Dad outside.

I head for the passenger seat, but he tosses the keys at me over the hood. I'm so surprised, I fumble, almost dropping them.

"You're letting me drive?"

He shrugs. "Been a while since you've had any practice."

A grin breaks across my face. Alright. Part of me is frantically coming up with ways this could go wrong—the crack still there on the passenger side of the windshield reminds me that driving with Dad is no picnic—but the rest of me is too excited to care. I love the power I feel behind the wheel of the car, the purr of machinery beneath my feet. It'll be even better when I have my license instead of a learner's permit and I can drive off on my own, radio blasting.

"Are we going anywhere in particular?" I ask, walking around and unlocking the driver's side door.

Dad shakes his head. "I figured we'd check out the town. You haven't seen much of it."

What I have seen hasn't made a great impression, but I'm not stupid enough to start complaining when Dad seems to be in a semi-decent mood. I slot the keys into the ignition and turn. The truck rumbles to life around me, and I hastily latch my seatbelt. Dad doesn't bother with his.

"Reverse," he tells me, like I'm dumb enough to drive forward and crash into the house.

Narrowly resisting the urge to roll my eyes, I back out of the driveway and onto the dirt road. Slow and steady. I'm not sure what the speed limit is around here, but it can't be that high. There's no one else driving, either, so there's no harm in being cautious. I gradually pick up speed as the house disappears in my rearview mirror. A huge weight lifts from my chest the second it's out of sight. I have to resist the urge to gun it, putting as much distance between myself and the house as possible. Instead, I come to a rolling stop at a crossroads.

"Left or right?" I ask Dad. I know from my trips into town that a left will take us toward the main road. I assume taking the right would just lead deeper into the neighborhood. Still, it's always better to ask, with Dad. No telling what he'll choose to take personally. He tells me to go left.

The speed limit in town is a depressingly slow 25 miles per hour. We crawl down the main road, past the shack where I got breakfast burritos the other day, the library, the cemetery, the gas station, the park where I cried. It's weird to think how many memories I've already made, despite never wanting to be here in the first place.

"Does anyone even use trains anymore?" I ask as I drive past the seemingly abandoned station. Dad just shrugs.

We get to the Walmart I've never managed to make it to. It's smaller than the one back home, and the garden section plants outside look like they haven't been watered in weeks. Dad tells me to pull into the parking lot, and he has me park the truck in a bunch of different spots, just to practice. He doesn't yell at me once, even when I pull too far forward into one spot and nearly crash into a stray shopping cart.

"Hey, look—a bulldog!" Dad's face lights up as he points out a brown and white bulldog panting in the backseat of a nearby car. Thankfully, there's a window rolled down. The dog has its head sticking out, and its slick tongue is lolling. Slobber trails down the side of the car door.

"Look at all that drool!" I can't help but laugh, and Dad joins in.

"Reminds you of Brisket, huh?" he says, and I nod. Dad looks wistful. "He was a good dog."

"Yeah."

"Tell you what, kid—when I hit it big, I'll buy you another one. How about that?"

I swallow down anger. For a moment there, things were almost pleasant between us, and of course he has to go and mention gambling. But he's looking at me expectantly, and I know, in his own worthless way, that he's being sincere. He really does think he'll hit it big one day and buy me a dog. He thinks that would make me happy. He probably even thinks he's a good dad.

Just for the moment, I decide it'd be easier to share his delusion.

"What would we name him?" I ask.

"I was thinking we'd get two, call 'em Chimi and Changa."

I snort.

We walk around Walmart to kill time, and Dad points out other stupid things he could blow money on, if he had any. A fancy grill. A giant flat screen TV. A trampoline. It's almost fun to play along. It reminds me of being a little kid, before I knew better, and I trusted everything he said. Kid-me used to beg my parents for a trampoline.

When we get back to the car, Dad takes the driver's seat, and I slide into place beside him. We've seen all there is to see in Claudesville, so I'm expecting him to head home, but instead he pulls onto an exit ramp and speeds down the highway.

"Where are we going?" I ask, surprised.

"I remember seeing a sign for an IHOP a few towns back on the drive in. I figured we'd go there for dinner. You and your sister are always saying how much you want to go to IHOP."

I bite my tongue. If there's one thing Maria Elena and I agree on, it's that IHOP sucks. In fact, we hate it so much, it's an inside joke. Every time we go out to dinner as a family, whenever we leave, one of us will slap our foreheads and go, "We should've eaten at IHOP!" Leave it to Dad to completely miss the point. But, because I've decided to live in La-La Land for the day, I keep all this to myself. He thinks he's doing something nice for me. Why burst his bubble?

We drive for like an hour, not speaking, but the radio keeps the silence from getting too oppressive. Dad has it tuned in to a rock station, and even though it's mostly old man stuff, I don't mind. I can't remember the last time I spent time with my dad and could honestly say I didn't mind.

When we get to IHOP, Dad orders a platter of greasy whatevers and I pick the least offensive pancakes I can find. Just as I'm taking my first bite, he says, "There's something I need to tell you when we get back home."

The pancake drops down my throat like a rock, and butter pecan syrup glues my mouth shut. Good thing I wasn't enjoying this meal anyway.

I swallow hard. "Why can't you tell me now?"

His eyes darken. "Trust me, it's bad news."

As opposed to all the good news we've been having lately. It's on the tip of my tongue to say something horrible, or to point out that I *don't* trust him, but I stay quiet.

Dad doesn't try to make conversation for the rest of the meal, and the drive back to Claudesville seems to take a million years. There's no relief as we pull up to the house. I feel nauseous at the sight of it. My bedroom window is still open, with that branch growing inside, but Dad doesn't notice. He's got his head down, and he walks with his shoulders drawn in, like he's tensing for a blow. Once we're inside, he takes a long time locking the door and carefully hanging his keys before finally turning to face me.

"Your mother's dead."

Chapter Eleven

It takes a while for the words to have meaning.

"I don't believe you," I tell him, my voice surprisingly steady.

How many times have I gotten this speech from Dad?

Your mom's gone. She's never coming back. She might as well be dead. Move on.

"She's not dead," I insist. "Just missing."

"No." Dad rubs the back of his neck. "She's dead. They found the body."

I shake my head. My neck twitches. "What body?"

"*Her* body."

I shake my head harder. "It wouldn't be her body. It's someone else's. How would you know? You didn't see it. It has to be somebody else's—it has to!" I don't even realize that I'm screaming until my own voice echoes back at me.

"She had her ID on her."

I just shake my head, no, no, no. For some stupid reason, I think of the tree branch upstairs tapping *yes*.

Dad reaches toward me. I flinch, but he only sets a hand on my shoulder. Still, I can't keep my teeth from chattering, and I tense beneath his touch. "She was living in a tent city out in New Mexico. A few of her homeless friends brought her to the hospital. They claimed they weren't doing any drugs, but—"

None of these words make sense. Tent city. Hospital. Drugs. *Dead.* None of them have anything to do with my mother, who loved me more than anything, who never would have left unless she had to. My mother, who's gone, but has to be coming back…

My father puts his arms around me, and I'm too weak to push him away. His touch feels like static against my skin.

Somehow, we make it to my room. I'm sitting on my bed, still unmade from last night, and Dad is standing nearby with his arms folded. He either doesn't notice the giant tree branch coming in through the window or doesn't care.

I hear noise. It takes a moment to realize that the noise is music, a song I love but will never want to hear again: "Amo, Amo" by Fuegoluz. My ringtone. My phone. It buzzes on the bedside table. I reach for it in my head but my arm doesn't move. My dad picks it up for me, listens.

"It's your sister," he says, holding the phone out to me. I watch my hand wrap around it. "I told her to call you. I figure the two of you have a lot to talk about."

"Hey, Francisca," says Maria Elena quietly. I hate the way she says my name, overenunciating each syllable like she's either scared to get it wrong or expects praise for getting it right. It's just a name. Even the sound of her voice annoys me, though it lacks her usual peppiness. "Dad says he told you about Mom."

It's as if a switch flips in my head. Before I'm aware of what I'm doing, I'm on my feet, screaming into the phone. "How do *you* know? Did he tell you first?" I hyperventilate. "You always get everything first! Everything's always about you!"

"You be nice to your sister!" Dad yells.

I laugh bitterly. "You're his favorite. You've always been his favorite."

"I know you're hurting right now, but this isn't exactly easy for me, either," says Maria Elena, annoyed. "We should—"

We. There's no *we.* There wasn't any we when Dad started taking her to all those pageants after Mom left. There wasn't any *we* when dad made me sell most of my stuff so we'd have room for Maria Elena's in the moving van. There's them on one side, Dad and Maria Elena, and then there's me. Me and my mother. *Mine.*

I only realize I've said all of this out loud—at the top of my lungs—when I hear Maria Elena sniffle into the phone and say, "She was my mother, too, you know," before hanging up.

The phone goes dead in my hand, and my anger evaporates as suddenly as it came. I feel empty. Not mad, not guilty, not sad. Just blank. A part of me recognizes that it wasn't fair to lash out at Maria

Elena like that. I'm just like Dad; the only difference is, I use words instead of hands.

Dad. Suddenly, the anger's back.

I turn to face him. "You knew. How long did you know?" A hysterical laugh explodes out of me. "You knew all day, didn't you? That is *sick!*" I scream. Tears burn my eyes. "You let me drive, and joked about dogs, and tried to make me happy while knowing that my mom was dead! You made me betray her memory! You—you—"

"I can't do anything right, can I." Dad's voice is flat. "Even when I try to do something nice for you, you turn it against me. Do you know why I took you out today?" His voice raises slightly. "My dad died when I was around your age. I know what it's like. There's a before and an after. I'll be damned if I'm the bad guy for giving you a few more hours of before. You'll thank me later."

I'm shaking with rage. "I—will—*never*—thank—you." I break down sobbing. "You beat her! None of this would have happened if you hadn't chased her away! This is all because of you! You killed her! I hate you, I hate you, I hate you!"

Dad opens his mouth, then closes it. Slowly, he turns and walks away, closing the door behind him.

Trembling, teeth chattering, I keep talking to the door.

"I hate you, I hate you, I hate you…"

Wind sighs through the orange tree. I don't even realize that I've been clenching my phone all this time until I see it fly through the air, striking the window with a *crack*.

"I hate you, too!" I shriek. "I hope you're stuck here suffering forever. You and me both, chica! You want to haunt me? I'll haunt you right back. I'll burn your stupid tree to the ground!"

It occurs to me that I don't even know if we have a lighter in the house, but whatever. I'll kill that tree one way or another. Will killing the tree even do anything to the ghost? Do ghosts feel pain? I sure hope so.

I'm having the kind of thoughts you know don't make sense even as you're thinking them, but I cling to crazy like a shield. I don't want to think about Mom, or Dad, or Maria Elena—anything that has to do with me and my life. The ghost thing, though—that I can handle.

Like a vision from the gods, an image of the big, white container of bleach under the bathroom sink pops into my mind. Pouring that on the tree's roots ought to do it. I take a step forward.

That is, I *try* to take a step forward, but somehow a blanket is wrapped around my legs. I stumble, grabbing onto my chipped bedside table to catch my balance. I glance down and notice that the blanket isn't just tangled: it's knotted. Tightly.

"Oh, real mature!" I snarl at the ghost, ripping through the knot. "You think it's funny, watching me fall? We'll see who's laughing when I poison you!"

Then, even though it was as clear as could be moments ago, I hear rain strike my window. The orange tree's branches scratch insistently at the glass. A low wind moans. A familiar voice whispers my name.

My blood runs cold.

"Mom?" I whisper back. I stay silent, but all I hear is the gathering storm outside. Thunder rumbles in the distance.

Tears well up, and I hate myself for it, but I hate the ghost even more.

"How dare you use her voice against me?" I scream, swiping at my eyes.

Then I clench my hands into fists, as if all I have to do is convince my body that I'm angry and the grief and fear and everything else will go away. I stomp toward the door, determined to get to the bathroom.

The door won't open. I yank on the handle, and the lights flicker off. The wind shrieks louder than ever, and branches batter the window.

"Leave me alone!" I shout toward the tree, pulling the doorknob as hard as I can. The door flies open, and I stumble into the hall. The only sliver of light comes from the door to my dad's room, and the sight of it makes me sick. I throw on the hall light just so that one patch of brightness in the dark will stop mocking me. It flickers, of course, but I don't care.

I storm into the bathroom and tear open the cabinet under the sink. There it is: the bleach. I sling it up one-handed, dropping it with a thunk onto the counter, breathing heavily. I catch my reflection in the mirror. A wild stranger looks back, and the bleach bottle shines like a star beneath the jittering bathroom light. It's blindingly, mesmerizingly white. I stroke the bottle. I love it. It's the answer to all my problems. All I have to do is pour it onto that tree—

—or—

No.

Yes.

How much would it take? Not much, right? And I'd barely even feel it if I went fast enough.

No.

No more. No more walking on tiptoes around Dad, always holding myself back. No more comparing myself to Maria Elena and coming up short. No more distance and depression. No more haunted house, no more ghosts. No more missing my mom, no more *"she's dead. They found her body."*

"There's a before and an after," Dad told me.

Shows what he knows. I can end "after" right here.

No, no, no, I tell myself, but my hands, unscrewing the cap of the bleach bottle, are going yes, yes, yes.

And the no's are getting fainter. It's hard to hear anything now, with the wind and rain outside, and the thunder, and the pounding in my chest, in my head, and all I want is to drown all of it out, and the shiny white bottle in my hands is full of liquid quiet, and I can't think, I don't want to, and I—

I throw the bottle as hard as I can. Bleach splashes up the side of the bathtub. I grasp my face with both hands, gasping, tasting chemicals in the air, and slowly drag my fingernails down my cheeks.

"No," I tell myself quietly, but there's a sinking feeling in my heart. I've resisted, for now, but when the urge keeps coming, giving in seems almost inevitable. It feels like there's only one way to escape, but now it's dripping down the drain.

I need to calm down. I have the idea of splashing cold water on my face, so I try to turn the sink on. The faucet is stuck, like the door handle was earlier. I close my eyes and count to ten. The ghost is trying to provoke me, but I've given it enough of a show for tonight. No more screaming and crying. I won't give her the satisfaction.

The second time I turn the handle, the faucet sputters on. A few drops of tepid water piddle out. I grab the handle and twist it as far as I can. Water explodes from the faucet in a torrent of white, but, as I stick my hands under the stream, it turns red. I yank my hands back, eyes darting across my palms, searching for cuts. Nothing. The red water flows faster and faster, overflowing from the sink basin and onto the pale brown tiles of the floor. Suddenly, it transforms into gashed-open flesh, oozing blood.

I shriek, jumping back. Then I blink and there's nothing more than a splash of water on the floor. The sink drain is closed. With a trembling hand, I reach through the water—ordinary, lukewarm water—and pull it open. There's a rattling groan from the pipes as the water is sucked down. At least, I tell myself it's just the pipes. Still, once the sink is off and all the water drained, I stand in the bathroom, shivering, unable to move.

I close my eyes. I need to get out of here.

I rush for the bathroom door, but I hear the hissing laughter of the wind as the lock clicks shut. I seize the handle, but it's slick—with blood?—and I can't get a good grip on it. I wipe my shaking hands on my pajama pants, grit my teeth, and grab it again. The lights flicker. The wind howls. The bathroom reeks of rotting oranges. I catch sight of my reflection out of the corner of my eye and see, not myself, but a grinning corpse.

I push and pull the door until it opens. I spill into the hall. Weeping, on my knees, I crawl back to my room. It's dark. A flash of lighting illuminates the disorder inside. I make it to bed. The sheets and blankets are snarled on the floor, so I sit on the bare mattress. I wrap my arms around my knees, shaking and crying and hating myself for it. Rain pounds through the open window. I let it hit me, shivering.

Eventually, the tears ebb away, but the rain keeps coming. It's all around me, not just slanting in through the window, but rolling off the spreading branch overhead. The orange is still there, gleaming wetly, hanging before my eyes like a full moon. Right within reach. I know there's death in the fruit of that tree, and it would be so, so easy...

I fall back onto the bed, closing my eyes. I tell myself I won't do it. I've already fought this battle once tonight, and I don't want to do it again. Ever again. But what if I'm trapped as long as I live?

Rain washes over me, and I imagine drifting away. Maybe it'll be sweet and painless. My nose is still prickling from the scent of bleach, and my neck itches with phantom rope burn. In comparison, it doesn't seem like such a bad way to go out, eating an orange.

But I can't bring myself to pick it. I don't know that it'll be painless, for one thing. It could be that I take one bite and fall asleep forever, but it could also be the most excruciating death-by-poison imaginable. And I'm tired. So tired. The idea of lifting my arms for anything is absurd. Maybe I'll die like this, just lying in bed. It won't be quick, but it seems easy enough.

Or, who knows, the feeling could pass.

I remember one day in ninth grade—I wore barrettes, which might as well have been a declaration of war to the boys-will-be-boys boys, the kind that bruise you up during lunch and get away with it because they play varsity. It hurt, all right. My back ached from being slammed against the locker, and my scalp tingled where they'd ripped out hairs by tearing off the barrettes, but the worst thing was knowing why they did it, and knowing just how many people—my dad included—would probably think they were in the right.

So, walking home, I had the bright idea of just running into traffic. I didn't do it, but the rush of every passing car sent a jolt through me, and I thought about it. I pictured it hard. I even convinced myself I could feel that initial impact, as if imagining the pain would take away some of the sting.

But later that night, Tia Lola picked me up to go to a poetry slam, and I had the time of my life. I snapped and cheered, and that afternoon with the cars and the boys felt a million years away.

The feeling could pass. It could happen. The thing is, it always comes back. It hangs over your head like a guillotine. Even when the blade's far away, you know it's there, waiting.

I don't want to wait anymore, and I don't have to.

I sit up slowly, but before I can even reach out, the orange drops from the branch. It doesn't fall, though. It levitates at eye level, then lowers slightly. The peel comes away in one long curl. My mom used to peel oranges like that. She used to feed me orange slices when I was sick. That's what I think about as the orange splits into segments. I part my lips, and softness touches my tongue. I bite down—an explosion of citrus. I close my eyes as the juice slithers down my throat.

Maybe I'm having fever dreams, and I'll wake up eight years old with my mom's hand on my forehead and my skin on fire. But the thing I hope for most as I go to sleep is that I won't wake up at all.

Chapter Twelve

Darkness first.

A rotting darkness surrounds me, scratching my skin. I'm torn open, gasping and cold like a gutted fish, and a tower rises from the gaping wound in my chest. No, not a tower—a tree. Growing. It drives its roots through my flesh, shattering bone, and thrusts itself into the earth. My head takes root, and my fingers and toes. I feel them lengthen and divide. The roots spread. I sense them digging into the distance.

Crack. Crack.

Decaying wood splinters. A coffin breaks open. Then another, and another. The roots worm into the throats of corpses, and dead voices cry out in the leaves above me.

Girasol.

Maria Elena!

A laughing girl.

A crying baby.

A woman's scream.

And me.

A root has grown through my throat, too. It curls inside me, bursting through my lips and scraping my tongue. I taste dirt and blood as my voice joins the awful chorus, raggedly screaming the words I can't speak for myself.

Mom! Mom, where are you? Help me! Mom!

Then, just as I feel a slender root prod my heart—

I know it's a dream because my mom calls me Francisca.

I didn't come out until she had already been gone for years, but, still, it feels right. I've always felt like she would have accepted me, if she knew. Not like my dad. No, Mom's biggest disappointment would probably be that I wasn't girly *enough* and she didn't have another daughter she could doll up like Maria Elena. But, time and time again, I've imagined my mother holding me close and whispering my name. She always knew me better than anyone, loved me without question. She, of all people, would understand who I truly am.

"Francisca," my mother says, beaming. "Look at what your grandma sent you!"

It's my dollhouse, white, spectacular, and whole, all gables, and turrets, and porches, and tiny, elegantly crafted pieces of furniture upholstered in pale rose. I reach toward the pretty blonde mother-doll with a small, chubby hand. I'm six years old again, the age I was when abuela died, when she left me the dollhouse in her will.

"There's no way she meant for you to have it," my father's voice rumbles from behind me just as my fingers stroke the mother-doll's long, sunshiney hair. "She was old—she's lost it. She must have meant it for Maria Elena."

"Maria Elena's too old for a dollhouse," my mother laughed, tossing her head. She lays a soft hand on my shoulder. "Believe me, she's much happier with all that jewelry your mom left her."

I hear grumbling and receding footsteps as my father leaves. I don't miss him, not while my mother is smiling softly at me as if I'm the most precious thing in the world, not when she hands me another doll, a black-haired little girl in a light yellow dress.

"What are you going to name her?" she asks.

I beam. "Luna, the nicest name in the world!"

As I tuck Luna into bed, I hear a subtle wail, a whimper of the wind. I turn to the window as if expecting to see someone, but the only thing there is the brilliant morning sun.

"A puppy!" I shriek, holding out my arms as my mother sets a chunky, wrinkled little dog in my lap. He's brindled, white and dark brown, and there's a red ribbon tied around his neck. He pants, then licks my cheek. "For me?"

My mother smiles, crinkling her eyes. We're at the park by our old house. The sunlight comes down through a canopy of leaves, making her eyes seem more green than blue. Behind her, children in party hats scamper across bright blue monkey bars, barrel down a twisty yellow slide, kick and scream on red tire swings. There's a picnic table nearby, heaped with presents, a slow cooker, a chocolate cake. "Happy birthday, Francisca."

I decide to name the dog after my favorite food, the birthday dinner my mom's prepared for me.

"His name is Brisket!" I declare, patting his head. "Brisket Fuentes!"

Leaves rustle overhead, gently at first, then urgently. The sunny sky darkens. A fat raindrop drips down my nose. Brisket lifts his head, tongue lolling to catch the rain. I laugh and stick my tongue out, too. Thunder breaks. I hear a voice calling in the distance: "Francisca! Francisca!"

It's a voice I've heard before, but it doesn't belong to anyone I know. I lift my head to respond, but before I can say a word, I'm in my old bedroom, and my mom is handing me a half-size violin, a light little bow.

"I know you've been wanting to take guitar lessons, like Maria Elena, but trust me when I say the violin is even more beautiful," she tells me, smiling even as I rake my bow across the strings, producing a grating screech.

I'm only seven, but a memory I shouldn't have yet comes to mind.

"She only bought you that stupid thing because she found it at a yard sale for twenty bucks," my dad sneers, yanking the fraying bow from my hand. "Piece of junk like that, they should've been paying *us* to take it off their hands."

"Francisca!" The voice is back, louder now. Thunder rolls. Rain crashes against the window as wind roars. "You have to get out! Your mother—"

My dolls are strewn across the floor, the pretty mother and little Luna, half of her hair hacked off from the time I tried to give her a haircut like Tia Lola's friend, Dolores. For just a moment, Luna seems to have moles on her cheeks, a sunflower behind her ear—

"Go, go, go!" my mother chants, her hand on my back as I bike forward.

I don't know why we're outside right now, in the middle of a thunderstorm, but I'm too happy to question it. Finally, after months of pleading, I have a bike of my very own. It's not new, or yellow, like I wanted, but it doesn't have training wheels, either. It's a big kid bike, like Maria Elena's, but without the stupid white wicker basket she tied onto the handlebars.

"Francisca!" the wind seems to sob. "Listen to me! Your mother—"

Lightning arcs through the sky, flashing across my mother's face. Her smile is gone. Her blue eyes are black. Blood mixes with rainwater and slithers down her hollow cheeks. The hand on my shoulder is nothing but bones held together by twitching chunks of sinew.

I scream.

"Boo!" my mother laughs, holding a bowl of gummy worms. She's dressed as a zombie for Halloween, her blonde hair spray-painted gray, her face painted with streaks of brownish-red. She's wearing a red velvet dress she got at the thrift store, then tore in places to make it seem like it's falling apart. Heavy eyeliner circles her eyes, making the blue seem paler than usual.

I laugh, feeling silly for getting scared. It's just my mom—of course it is. She always goes all out for Halloween.

"We're almost done setting up the haunted house," she tells me with a smile. But, when I look behind her, instead of seeing the cheerful, yellow house I grew up in, the one she always festooned with fake cobwebs and animatronic spiders, it's the new house in Claudesville, the one with the orange tree. The windows are broken, and wind rushes through them, screaming. Rain sloughs off my mother's makeup, and, with it, her flesh.

"Don't be scared," says my mother's grinning skull. She pats my shoulder with a skeleton hand. "Come here, Francisca," she whispers, barely audible over the shrieking wind, the clattering of her bones. "Give your mother a hug."

I start to raise my arms, but I'm tackled from behind.

"Francisca, don't!" screams the wind, a voice in my ear.

I kick, and shove, and I find myself sprawled under a girl in the wet dirt beneath the orange tree. She's pale, panting. And familiar.

There's a sunflower tucked behind her ear.

"You!" I shout, pushing her off me. "You're the ghost that's been haunting me!"

She shakes her head, her braid twitching like a snake. "You don't understand!" she cries as lightning flashes. "It's your mother. *She's* the one that was—"

I snarl. Who does this ghost think she is—invading my dreams, accusing my mother? "I told you to leave me *alone!*"

"I'm trying to protect you!"

"*I'm* trying to protect you, Francisca," says my mother, alive and beautiful again. Rain slips down her cheeks like shining tears. "I'm here now, and I know a way that we can be together forever." She's still holding out her arms, waiting for me to return her embrace.

I stand slowly, not bothering to brush the dust off my legs. The dead girl grabs me by the wrist with a wet, clammy hand. I pry her thin fingers off me without turning to look.

"This is my mother," I tell her, filled with calm at the sight of my mother's smiling face, her open arms. She's come back for me, just like I always knew she would. I'm nothing like the dead girl, trapped and alone. Her father killed her mother. She killed herself. Not me. I have everything I want right here. "You can't keep me away from her just because you've lost your chance of ever seeing yours again."

The dead girl gasps as if she's been stabbed. "Francisca—"

"Francisca," my mother coos, wrapping her arms around me. "There's my good girl." Then she laughs, a high, piercing laugh that shatters my calm like lightning tearing through the sky. Her grip tightens. Her skin rots, dissolves, pools into an inky black puddle at our feet. Rain feeds into it, making the blackness rise until it's up to my ankles, my knees, my neck. Before it reaches my eyes and drags me into utter darkness, I have just enough time to hear the dead girl cry out once more.

PART TWO:

MUERTA

Chapter Thirteen

I have been dead for a hundred years, and now the girl who shares my name just might share my fate.

It is all my fault. I coaxed the orange into being, the fruit of the tree of death, in the hopes that she would eat it and allow me to enter her dreams. I only wanted to communicate with her. It has been a long and lonely century, and her spirit burned bright. I believed that she would help me, if she only knew how.

I tried to tell her who I was. I wrote my name on the bathroom mirror, which she mistook for her own. I told the story of my sister, Maria Elena, through dolls. I've passed on sensations—unfortunately, few of them pleasant—so that she might understand. I've gazed at her through the dark eyes of sunflowers, begging to be seen in return.

And now I have doomed her. A stronger ghost than myself followed her here—a malevolent, grasping spirit. She has shattered glass and made the sink run red with blood. She has drawn the girl toward the basement of my own long-dead nightmares, blending them with the horrors of another, less distant past. I should have known better than to offer the orange, knowing it would weaken the barrier between life and death.

I am responsible for my sister's death and my own, but I will not be responsible for hers. Whatever it takes, I will help her return to the Land of the Living. I will follow her down whatever dark paths the ghost of her mother drags her, for it is my fault that path was open.

Without a moment's hesitation, I throw my hand on what was once the live girl's shoulder, on what is now nothing but writhing, viscous black mass. The darkness leaps up my arm, cold, heavy, and slimy. It bears down on my flesh, coats my eyes, drags me lower, lower, lower. I sink as blackness coils around me.

I am aware of the live girl in flashes—for fleeting instants, her terror and confusion become my own. Then the impressions fade and I am myself again. I sense flailing limbs, gritted teeth, desperate motion. She is fighting, struggling to break free from whatever dark substance has consumed us. Whatever power is at work is greater than my own; I let it take me where it will.

Suddenly, I am on my knees on the cracked, dusty earth beneath the orange tree, gasping and trembling.

I am beneath the orange tree, gasping and trembling, as Maria Elena lays motionless beneath a tangle of broken branches, twigs and leaves snarled in her loose brown curls.

"No!" I shriek, lunging toward her lifeless form.

Her glassy eyes are wide open, reflecting me back at myself. I am alone. I will always be alone…

The body shifts; the branches vanish. The live girl kneels before me, retching and moaning.

"Francisca" I reach toward her, but she crawls forward and vomits what looks like a torrent of ink. It splatters the ground, then sinks into the dirt, leaving no trace. She groans and drops with a thud.

I will not lose her, not in the place my sister died.

I seize the girl's hand. Her fingers jerk against mine. "Francisca, get up," I tell her, trying to sound strong even as my voice shakes. "Francisca!"

Her eyelids flicker open. "Mom?" she croaks.

"No, it's me." I hesitate before giving her my name. "Francisca Flores."

She shoves me away, glaring. "What are you doing here?" She squints around. "Where's Mom? Wha—" Her eyes widen as her gaze slips past me, toward the house.

I turn, too. The house wavers in and out of focus, distorted and immaterial, quivering like a soap bubble. Its edges are transparent, but the windows are white, opaque. Tiles vanish from the rooftop only to suddenly reappear. Cracks in the stucco materialize then fade. It appears to be caught in time, vacillating between the way it appeared when I was alive and the way it looks in the present. Only the sky above is unchanging: a flat and baleful gray.

Above us, oranges brighten sharply, glowing like suns. The girl and I are glowing as well—a more muted radiance, like moonlight filtered through clouds. I stare at my hands, watching them appear to solidify only to fade away. Even when they are in focus, I can no longer make out the lines on my palms, the blue web of veins, the fine hair on the backs of my hands. Is the problem with my eyes or the rest of me? I reach for the sunflower in my hair; I can feel its dry petals, but only just.

"I do not know where we are, or how to get out, but I am going to help you escape," I promise.

The girl snorts. "Great. Sounds like you really know what you're doing." She stands, brushing dirt off her legs as she scowls down at me, still on my knees. "Why should I trust you, anyway? You've been haunting me all this time!"

"So has your mother," I say earnestly. "You have to believe me. She—"

She narrows her eyes and leans down close. "My mother would *never* do this to me!" she hisses. "I don't care if you're dead, undead, or what. Say anything like that to me again, and I will punch your lights out."

I let out a shaky breath. "I could be mistaken," I say at last. "Maybe the ghost only looks like your mother. It could have disguised itself to win your trust. Look around," I add, rising to my feet. "If your mother loves you, would she have brought you to a place like this?"

Some of the anger fades from the girl's eyes as she studies the bleak world around us.

"I don't think so," she says in a low voice. "Maybe you're right." She drops into a crouch, clasping her head with both hands. "Oh, God, where am I? Is this the Land of the Dead? Am I dead?" Her breathing quickens, and I instinctively place a hand on her back.

"I don't think so," I say softly, trying to reassure us both. "I have never been to the Land of the Dead, but I think, if I reached it, I would feel at peace. Even now, there is something missing within me."

The girl lifts her head, the tracks of tears glistening on her round cheeks in the orange light. "Then where are we?"

"Wherever we are, we're here together, and I'm going to help you get home."

She regards me with tearful suspicion. "Why?"

"I sense this is a space between life and death," I say slowly. "The boundaries are weak around our house because of my presence. It would not have been possible for your—the ghost that *looks* like your mother to bring you here if not for me. I never meant to hurt you," I add in a gentler tone. "I never meant to hurt anyone." Except for myself.

She gives me a hard stare, then sighs. "I still don't know if I trust you, ghost girl, but you seem all right."

"Thank you, Francisca."

"We can't both be Francisca," she says. "That's gonna get confusing fast."

I nod, toying with the end of my braid. "For the most part, I've been calling you 'the alive girl' in my head."

The girl tips her head from side to side, considering. "It has a nice ring to it. Oh! I've got it!" Her face lights up, and it's a surprise to see. Until this point, I have only ever seen her sad, scared, or sullen. "You can call me Francisca Viva—Viva, for short." Then she frowns. "I guess that makes you Muerta. That seems kind of rude."

"I don't mind," I say quickly—too quickly. Although I've had plenty of time to get used to the notion, I still do not like thinking of myself as dead.

Viva shrugs. "All right. Muerta, then. What do we do now?"

I open my mouth to respond—to say what, I have no idea— when a sudden, hot wind howls.

Dust billows upward, coalescing into faceless figures. Wind-women fling out provocative skirts of sand as they swirl down the street. Wind-children sprint past, shrieking and laughing. Men of the wind whistle mournfully from treetops, shaking blooms from branches. The oranges above tremble but do not fall.

"What...are they?" Viva pants.

The wind goes silent. The figures stop. Slowly, they turn their heads toward Viva and me. A wrenching howl rattles the tree branches as they surge toward us. Blazing dust stings my eyes. I throw up my hands, but they offer no protection; the sand passes through them. Viva screams.

Then I feel a tug on the back of my neck. Hot dust crumbles down my back as I am pulled to my feet.

"Get inside," a low, familiar voice murmurs. "Hide."

The figure has pulled Viva up with its other hand. It pushes us toward the open door with a warm gust of wind. For a moment, indistinct features form on its face: holes for eyes, a protrusion for a nose. Then they sink back into nothingness. I reach for its hand—to thank it? to try to bring it inside with us?—but its fingers crumble to dust. The door slams shut behind us as the house groans in the wind.

It's my house: I recognize the ofrenda heaped with fruit near the door, the red woven rug at our feet, the phonograph near the staircase.

Viva stares at me with wide, terrified eyes, and I shake my head in response to her earlier question. "I don't know what they are."

"Are we sure this isn't the Land of the Dead?" Viva asks, raising her voice. "Because those things seem pretty dead to me. There's definitely no way they're alive!"

"Trust me, they're not," a voice pipes up from the stairwell. The stairs creak as a dust-figure, seemingly more solid than the wraiths outside, descends. Its face is blurry, like a reflection in moving water, making it impossible to make out its features. But it *has* features. It holds out a broad hand of dust. "Pablo Flores-Fuentes. Welcome to my house."

Viva's jaw drops. "You're the one that died and left my dad the house—Paco Something!"

Something like annoyance ripples across its face. "That's *Pablo* Something. Pablo…" It drums its fingers on the banister, leaving a thick film of brownish-gray dust. "I forget."

"Flores-Fuentes," I say softly.

"Flores-Fuentes!" it cries. For just a moment, its face solidifies—a man's face, broad and beaming, with gray, whiskery cheeks and bright brown eyes. "Thanks for reminding me!" He plucks an orange from the ofrenda and bites into it, peel and all. "My favorite! I think."

Viva looks slightly sick. "You mean you don't know?"

Pablo's face grows sad, then it blurs. "You're in la tierra de los olvidados now, chica. It won't be long before you start forgetting, too."

"The Land of the Forgotten?" Viva gasps. "So I *am* dead!"

"I don't think so," Pablo replies, taking another juicy bite of orange. "You've got this strange little life-glow around you, but it's fading fast."

I take a deep breath. "We have to get you back to the Land of the Living."

"I don't get it." Viva clenches her jaw, deep in thought. "Why would that ghost pretend to be my mom, and why would it bring me here? We need answers." She reaches for the door.

I grab Viva's shoulder. "Don't!"

But it's too late. She wrenches the door open and leaps into the wailing wind.

I'm tempted to let her go. All she's done is lash out, accuse me, demand answers I have no way to give.

Then I see Maria Elena sprawled beneath the orange tree, eyes blank. Maria Elena, who would have jumped out that door right after Viva no matter how mad she was. Maria Elena, my radiant, fearless sister.

I race after Viva, following her into the maelstrom. At first, I can't see her. Then I hear her scream.

She's surrounded by dust-figures, their shapes blurring into one another, forming a wall of shifting sand that encircles her, howling. I can just make out her silhouette, dark within the blazing sand. She cries out again, and I try to reach for her, but I'm blown backward by the shrieking wind. My head slams against the wall. I feel every bump of stucco against the back of my skull. Then a memory overtakes me.

"What did you say to me?" he snarls in a low voice, leaning down so his sour-smelling mouth almost brushes my lips. His arms cage me to the wall, and my head throbs where he pushed me back.

My voice is quiet, and it trembles, but I manage to say, "Leave her alone."

He laughs, a drawn-out, ugly sound. The sun glints off the beginnings of a beard on his face, the pustules erupting on his forehead. "Brave little girl, aren't you?"

Behind him, I see Abril San Miguel, frozen. Abril the silent. Abril, the only friend I have left.

She's still in uniform—we all are. We are home at last, for one brief snatch of summer, but the residential school uniforms are still stiff against our skins, reminding us of dangers we could not leave behind, like the boy.

School was a nightmare for us all, a stone monolith hundreds of miles from anyone who loved us where we had the Spanish smacked from our mouths, but it was harder still for Abril. She could not speak any language. She lost the ability when Maya was killed by the same cruel stroke of fate that snatched my sister.

Abril was mocked by students and punished by teachers, but that was nothing compared to what the older boys did to her. She never told me—she could tell no one—but when I saw him grab her wrist, I knew. And I knew I had to stop it.

In the distance, the train whistle roars. With my eyes, I beg Abril to run. I don't want her to see what happens next.

And I don't want to remember it, either.

Chapter Fourteen

Through the haze of sand, I see Muerta get blown against the wall. Then I hear her whimper, her voice barely audible over the shrieking wind. "Leave her alone…"

She came outside to protect me—the same reason she tried to warn me in the dream, the reason she followed me here. Guilt and shame churn in my stomach as I watch Muerta sink to her knees, shaking. I've been nothing but cruel to her, but she's never stopped trying to help me. It isn't right.

The wind snatches the sunflower from Muerta's hair. She gasps and reaches for it, but it's sucked into the swirling cloud of dust that's closing in on me. Faces flicker through the sand for only a moment before transforming into new ones with ghoulish, gaping mouths and empty eyes. I see a spindly hand attached to no body coalesce from the cloud and close around Muerta's sunflower, stopping its wild, whirling dance and holding it over my head. One of its petals falls away; Muerta collapses, moaning.

I jump, seizing the flower. The hand breaks apart at my touch. The wind hisses as if angered, and the cloud closes in, but I grit my teeth and charge through it, holding the sunflower tight. Sand stings my eyes and sears my skin. I cry out as rough hands grab my ankles and throw me to the ground. I kick; they crumble. Crawling and panting, I make my way to Muerta as fast as I can and tuck the sunflower back behind her ear. She doesn't move.

Wind whips the sand into new shapes, stumbling figures that lurch toward us. As their legs dissolve beneath them, they slither on their stomachs, screaming silently with the voids of their mouths, the pits of their eyes.

I shake Muerta's shoulder. "C'mon. We've gotta get inside."

She screams at my touch and jerks away, trembling. "Abril, run!"

Abril—one of the girls from the dreams. I don't know why Muerta thinks I'm her, but there's no time to figure it out.

I snake one arm beneath Muerta's knees and wrap the other around her shoulder, hiking her up. She's almost weightless in my arms; only a slight, cool pressure lets me know she's there. I fight to open the door while keeping Muerta balanced and dodging the sand monsters' hands. I grind fingertips of sand to dust beneath my heel as I jiggle the lock, Muerta's head lolling against my shoulder. Just as I feel the wind's hot breath on the back of my neck, the door opens. Muerta and I spill inside. My nose is inches from a pair of grimy brown boots.

The boots clomp toward the door. I hear it slam shut. "Stay in or stay out! I won't have you girls tracking dirt everywhere—this house is messy enough as it is!" a male voice grips

"Pablo Flores-Fuentes," I remember.

His face solidifies, brightening at the sound of his name, before his features go blurry again. "That's right. And I don't think I ever got your names."

I sit up while Muerta stays face down on the floor. "Francisca, both of us. But you can call me Viva." Then I crawl over to Muerta and tap her shoulder. "Muerta? What's wrong?"

There's a million possible answers to that question. She might be having some kind of reaction to the dust-things outside, but she saw them earlier without passing out. Maybe she hit her head too hard when the wind pushed her into the wall? Did she get a concussion, and that was why she called me Abril earlier? Can ghosts even *get* concussions?

Slowly, Muerta lifts her head. Her eyes are emitting a strange pale glow, more intense than the faint grayish light that surrounds our bodies. I gaze into the light, and I catch glimpses of memory.

Summer sun. Rustling leaves. A train whistling in the distance. A girl wearing an old-fashioned school uniform. Black hair falls across her face, almost but not quite hiding eyes that are wide with fear. A hot, hard mouth forcing itself against mine.

I clench my eyes shut. When I open them again, I'm in the living room of the new house. The ofrenda and phonograph are gone; instead, there's the puke-orange couch I helped my dad carry in a life-time ago, and the coffee table stained with dark rings, bite marks on the legs where Brisket used to chew on them. Muerta is still staring forward with blank, glowing eyes.

"Muerta, hey," I tell her firmly, sitting her up. "Listen. It's just a memory. It's over now. You're here." *Here* is not a very comforting place to be, but I leave that part out.

For a moment, the glow flickers and her eyes seem to meet mine. Then she whimpers.

I grab her hands, squeeze as hard as I can. "Can you feel that?" I ask. "Squeeze back if you can feel that."

Slowly, gently, Muerta's fingers close around mine.

"Great!" I yell. "You're killing it, Muerta!" I grimace at myself. "Bad choice of words."

The corner of her mouth twitches.

"Is that what I have to do to distract you? Make a fool out of my-self? 'Cuz I'll do it," I ramble. "Just ask Cat and Angie—I embarrass myself all the time. One time, I choked on a hot dog at the bowling alley—" I cut myself off because the rest of that story involves me get-ting mouth-to-mouth from one of the guys who ran the snack counter, and that's probably the last thing Muerta wants to hear about right now. Plus, I'm not sure Muerta knows what a hot dog is, or a bowling alley, for that matter. "And there was this other time I had to give a pre-sentation in English, but I got the worst case of hiccups—"

I go on and on, gripping Muerta's hands as hard as I can, oc-casionally prompting her to squeeze back, or nod, or just give me some sign that she's paying attention. I have no idea if any of what I'm doing actually helps, or if the memory just fades on its own, but, gradually, Muerta comes out of it. Her eyelids flutter, and the glow dims.

"Thank you," she breathes.

I shake my head. "You tried to save me—it was the least I could do."

Muerta tries to stand, but she gasps and falls against me. I let her lean on me as I lead her to the couch. "You just lay down," I tell her. "We're safe here." I think.

Muerta closes her eyes, and I sigh, staring down at the dark fingerprints staining the arm of the couch. My dad left them while clawing for the remote with booze-soaked hands years ago, and I've stared at them countless times, during countless lectures. It'd be hard to find an item in the house that I *can't* associate with dad yelling at me, but, when I picture my dad's red-faced rage, I can also see his thick fingers digging into the arm of this couch, his body settled into its sagging cushions as the TV blares behind me. Muerta's braid dangles over the edge of the couch, and I move to tuck it under her head. My hand brushes the stain, and I'm thrust into a memory.

I thrust out my chin and raise my voice. "I don't care if you call me Francisca or not," I lie, clenching my hands into fists so my dad won't see them shaking. "I just don't want you to be surprised when other people do. It's who I am, and, if you can't respect that—" My voice breaks, and my neck jerks to the side. My tics were annoying at the best of times, but I especially hated them when I was trying to act strong and they let anyone who was watching me know just how nervous I really was. Still, I got the final word out. "Tough."

Dad doesn't bother to reply. At first, he just sinks deeper into the couch, his fingers tapping idly by the stain. His eyes are glazed over, and I can see the reflection of a football game in his pupils. It's as if I'm dead—no, as if I never existed in the first place. Eventually, he cranes his neck so he can peer around me to the TV, the only acknowledgement that I'm even there.

Shock crashes over me like icy water. I came prepared for a fight. My dad made no secret of his disgust toward trans people, so I knew defending myself would be an uphill climb. Even seeing a girl with short hair or a boy with earrings out in public was enough to set him off, and he could make any political conversation about "the gay agenda" no matter how unrelated it was to the topic. I memorized facts, statistics. I was ready to argue. More than that, I was ready to match anger with anger, to let my dad's fury kindle my own and shout as loud as I needed to make my voice heard.

I wasn't ready to be ignored.

It's as if what I'm saying is so ridiculous, it doesn't even deserve a response. My declaration is like the buzzing of a fly, the whining of gnat. He won't recognize me as a daughter, or even a son. His cold contempt is so unexpected, all I can do is stare at the stain on the couch, unable to meet my father's eyes, and shuffle out of the living room, twitching. My fire abandons me. I am nothing, no one.

I come out of the memory. I close my eyes. I never fought him again after that. Not really, not over anything that mattered. I argued, sure, and I talked back, but I always knew, deep down, that it was pointless. That I'd already lost.

A quiet yet cruel laugh echoes through the living room. I open my eyes and find my mother leaning in the doorway. Compared to all the dust-things outside, her features look painfully sharp—thin nose, diamond-shaped face, narrowed eyes. Her blonde hair is caked with blood, and black sludge oozes from the edges of her eyes. She takes a step toward me, the red sequins on her stiletto heels glinting wickedly.

This isn't my mom, no matter how much it looks like her. This is the ghost that broke into my dream and dragged me here, the one that's wearing her face to manipulate me. I ball my hands into fists. It won't work anymore.

"I don't know who you are, but you don't scare me!" I shout. Muerta murmurs and rolls onto her side at the noise, but her eyes remain closed. "I know you're not my mother!"

"No," she says softly, eyes glinting with hatred. The house rumbles around us. The lights flicker out as dark dust cascades from the ceiling. I open my mouth, but a rough hand of sand closes around my throat, choking me into silence. "You're not my *daughter*."

Glass shatters. The moaning of the wind is deafening. Scalding sand lashes through the darkness, shooting tendrils around my wrists and yanking me into the air. I scream, kicking wildly, but my feet don't make contact with anything.

"Viva?" Muerta's anxious voice calls out from behind me. "What's happening?"

Gritty fingers trail down my cheeks. "Viva, Francisca—call yourself whatever you want," says the ghost I refuse to believe is my mother. "*I* know who you really are." Fingernails cut my face. I inhale sharply, then gag on hot dust. "You disgust me."

I pant, clenching my eyes shut. This isn't my mom. My mom would never—

—would she?

I don't know. I was so young when she left, it's easy to assume the best of her, to focus on all the happy memories we shared, to imagine a perfect reunion, but, when it comes down to it…I really, truly don't know.

I stop breathing, stop fighting. This ghost might not be my mother, but that doesn't mean the one in my head is any more real, and what have I been fighting for, all this time, except a chance to see her again?

"Leave her alone!" Muerta shouts.

Her. That one syllable rekindles my fight. Sure, I want to be a daughter my mother would be proud of, but, more importantly, I want to be the kind of person *I* can be proud of. I'm Francisca Luna Fuentes, and I won't let anyone take that from me.

I kick as hard as I can, striking the ghost in the chest. It crumbles away like rotting wood beneath my foot, and tendrils of hissing sand rush around me. The moaning of the wind outside gets louder. The door trembles, then cracks open. Dust pours in, sometimes taking the shape of a racing body or slithering form, but, mostly, indistinct faces coalesce, then blend into new ones, then vanish entirely in the shifting sand.

Muerta seizes my hand. Everything stops.

A brilliant orange glow encases us both, and the sand retreats, shrieking. I feel grounded. I *feel.* For the first time since arriving in la tierra de los olvidados, I feel the pressure of my shirt against my shoulders, the pinch of my slightly too small black sneakers, the dry heat of the air on my skin. I can also sense Muerta's hand grow lighter in mine. Am I taking substance from her, or am I just now noticing her near-intangibility? I think she's changing; we're changing together.

Chapter Fifteen

I feel…lighter. Before, I was empty; now, I am filled with an orange radiance that lifts me off the ground and sends tingling warmth racing through my body. Meanwhile, Viva's hand feels heavier, more solid in mine. I can feel the ridges of her knuckles, a slightly raised scar on her palm near the base of her middle finger, fine hair on the back of her hand.

I stood up for Viva, just like I stood up for Abril in my memory. Yes, Maria Elena was brave, but I was brave, too, once. I had forgotten, all my courage stripped away by the press of that boy's lips.

My feet drift back to the floor, and the glow around us both fades.

Viva turns to me, dark eyes wide. "What just happened?"

I rub the back of my head. Somehow, this feels connected to the memory of Abril I had when the wind knocked me into the wall, but what is the link between that memory and the orange light, the orange light and the dust-things that were chasing us?

"The light seemed to frighten them away," I say slowly, "but why?"

"Who cares *why?*" Viva exclaims. "We just have to figure out how to do it again in case they come back! That, and we need to get out of here."

I seize Viva's shoulder. "You are not leaving the house again!" I cry, my voice more quivery than I would like it to be. "And if you do, I—I'm not going after you!" I fail to convince even myself that I mean it.

"I meant out of this place, the Land of the Forgotten," Viva explains.

I look away, embarrassed. "Oh."

Viva drums her fingers on the edge of the couch. I notice a dark stain almost like a handprint nearby. "When I touched that stain earlier, it triggered a flashback," she said in a low voice. "After that, we started glowing, and it scared the dust-things away…"

A pulse of excitement runs through me. "When I hit my head, I had a memory of Abril!" If Viva's having memories, too, if it's not just me…it can't be happening for no reason. "I think the light is connected to the memories, somehow," I say slowly. "Maybe the only way we can leave la tierra de los olvidados is if we start remembering certain things. That could be why the—the dust-things were scared of the light. Maybe it was taking us closer to life." Or death.

"We gotta stop calling them dust-things," says Viva, shaking her head. "They're way too scary to have a name that close to 'dust bunnies,' but who knows," she adds with a shrug. "They're scared of orange light—maybe they're scared of the vacuum, too."

"What should we call them, then?" I ask.

"They're olvidados," a male voice replies. "The forgotten."

I turn to see a faceless figure of dust descending the stairs, idly tossing and catching an orange with one hand. Each time, the orange sinks slightly into its palm, shedding grains of sand as it rises. A gaping mouth forms in the center of the dust-thing's head and takes a bite out of the orange.

"Pablo Flores-Fuentes!" I recall.

For a moment, a true face appears, and he smiles at me. Then there is only a wide mouth, ringed with sand darkened by rivulets of orange juice. He takes another sloppy bite. "The one and only," he says with his mouth full. "I started off like the two of you, but I guess sooner or later, I'll end up like *them*," he says, inclining his head toward the door.

I shiver.

"Well, *I* won't," says Viva with determination. "And neither will you," she adds, her fierce eyes latching onto mine. "We just have to find more memories, and then…"

"We go home," I say softly.

Viva snaps her fingers, then points at me. "Exactly! Home! Yes!" She lowers her head with a sigh. "Except we only discovered those memories by accident, and we don't know how or where to find more."

A harsh, wailing wind outside rattles the door. Viva and I glance at each other.

"I bet there's more memories upstairs," she says in a much higher voice than usual.

I nod vigorously. "Yes, let's start upstairs."

"Oh, don't mind me," says Pablo in a mournful tone, his mouth shaping into a frown. "I'll just stay here, languishing and forgotten. Alone. For eternity."

"You do that," Viva replies, pushing past him to leap up the stairs.

"Sorry!" I cry before following Viva. A part of me feels guilty, but Viva and I barely have any idea what we need to do to help ourselves; I can't even begin to know what would help Pablo.

At the top of the stairs, Viva drums her fingers on the banister, scanning the hall full of closed doors. "I guess the bedroom's as good a place as any to start," she says, opening the second door on the left. Viva takes one step forward, then pauses. "Muerta, is this your room?" she asks, turning over her shoulder.

I nod. Although the living room appeared as it does in Viva's time, the bedroom is mine. I trace the leaves painted on the doorway, willing myself to remember my mother's even strokes, her patient breaths, the reflection of my smile in her eyes. I remember it all, but the memory doesn't overtake me the way the recollection of Abril did outside.

While I linger in the doorway, Viva makes her way to my desk. There's an unlit candle within an elegant bronze cage that takes up nearly half the desk. My father made both years ago, when he was quick to smile and quicker with his hands. The thought of him makes me cold.

He killed my mother, and I died without ever knowing why.

"There's a lot of papers over here," Viva calls, pulling me back into the present.

Stacks of books with yellowing pages, leather-bound journals with cracked spines, and scrapbooks bursting with dried flowers tower precariously. Scattered around the stacks lie dull pencils, pens and an inkwell, brittlebush blossoms in a pot painted with matching yellow flowers, a bronze music box with a broken handle. One scrapbook is fanned open where I left it, revealing a page with preserved sunflowers and a pencil-sketched border of leaves.

"Maybe one of these will jog your memory?" Viva holds up a notebook I recognize as the one I used for school, and a single page flutters to the ground.

I kneel to pick it up, and nothing happens. "I guess I don't have strong memories of getting an 86 on an English test," I say, handing the paper back to Viva. I'm expecting her to put it back in the notebook, but, instead, she stares at it intently.

"Recollection," she murmurs. "Recollection!" Her face lights up, and she grabs my hand. "Look at this! Tell me what you see."

The word "recollection", which I incorrectly defined as "picking up something that was dropped or lost" is underlined in red, and beside it is the teacher's correction: "memory."

"It *is* odd that there was a question on memory," I say hesitantly, unsure what Viva's point is.

"Muerta, what if you were right?" Viva asks, her voice rising in excitement. "What if we literally have to *re-collect* memories by touching different things until we've gotten enough to go home?"

My eyes widen; Viva's theory explains why I remembered Abril after hitting the wall. "You might be right."

"You're the one who's right," Viva corrects, grinning. "It was your test that gave me the answer." Then Viva pulls my hand and yanks me over to the desk. "Quick, start touching things!" she exclaims, pressing my hand against books, the birdcage, potted plants.

"Viva, let go!" I exclaim, yanking my hand from her grasp.

"The faster we remember things, the faster we can get out of here," Viva snaps, fear in her eyes. "And it's your room, so it's not like touching anything will jog *my* memory."

She has a point. Still, I rub my wrist and shoot Viva a rueful glace before letting my fingers skim the smooth surface of my desk.

The wind shrieks, and there is the unmistakable sound of the door being wrenched open. The wailing grows louder, and a series of dull thumps come closer and closer. I peer out the door and see Pablo Flores-Fuentes shaking in the stairwell.

"Help!" he cries, his face shifting rapidly between an expression of horror and no expression at all. "The olvidados—they're in the house—"

"Muerta, close the door!" Viva shouts.

Before the memory of Abril, before the orange light, perhaps I would have listened to her. But, now, I know I am brave, and I will do what is right.

I hold the door open. "Hurry! Get inside!"

"Muerta!" Viva screams in frustration.

Pablo scrambles down the hall on all fours, his limbs little more than elongated sacks of sand—no hands, no feet—but his face is perfectly clear. He smiles, baring crooked teeth, and the corners of his eyes crinkle as he crawls through the doorway. "Thank you, Francisca."

"They're all coming inside!" Viva yells from the window. "Quick, close the door, before they—"

A shriek of laughter silences her, and a gust of scalding wind sweeps through the hall. Olvidados crystallize in the hot, dusty air. I see them for only a moment: gaping mouths, pits for eyes, desperate, reaching claws. Then they meld into a single cloud of sand, pressing closer. I try to shut the door, but the wind shoves me back. I crumple to the ground as a tornado of sand whirls into the room.

"Start touching things!" Viva has to shout to be heard over the wind. "The light—" She chokes on a mouthful of sand and sinks to her knees, but I know what she was trying to tell me. Our only chance to escape is if we can glow again, and the only way to glow is to unlock another memory. We think.

I race around the room, trying to dodge the swirling sand while dragging my hands on every available surface—the desk, the bed, the walls, the floors. Nothing. Meanwhile, the tornado rages on, tearing paintings and sketches from the walls, flinging books across the room, shattering my mirror. I see a small hand, a child's hand, tentatively reach for my music box, but Viva snatches it first and tosses it to me. Before I can catch it, the wind rips it away. It shatters through the window.

I don't know what to do. I don't know what I *can* do. The wind is doing everything in its power to keep me from touching anything, and what I have touched has failed to spark any memories. Maybe our theory was wrong. Maybe all we can do is wait until we crumble to dust…

Pablo, who had been cowering behind Viva, slowly straightens. As he stands, his limbs solidify, hands and feet coalescing at their ends. Then, between his hands, a series of folds materializes. He brings his hands together, and the folds press together, letting out a sound like a kicked dog. It's an accordion.

And then Pablo starts to sing. I can recognize the folk tune he is singing, but only just. His voice is awful, almost as terrible as the wailing of the olvidados, but more deafening, louder than the whimpering accordion. It sounds so horrible, olvidados start to howl with pain, creating wretched harmonies.

Pablo's face materializes, and I see eyes that glint with courage. He is trying to protect us, just like I tried to protect him by opening the door. A silent understanding passes between us as he raises his voice. I take Viva's hand and pull her into the room across the hallway, locking the door behind us. I doubt it will be strong enough to keep the olvidados out, but it's all I can think to do.

Viva scans the empty, cobweb-infested room. "Where are we?"

Trembling with fear, worrying for Pablo, I let out a sigh and sink to the ground. "My mother's studio," I say tiredly. "At least, it used to be."

This room may give us a moment of respite from the olvidados, but it is barren: there is nothing inside to trigger my memory, no trace of my mother, or the girl I used to be. Then I see a lone paintbrush wedged in the grout between two tiles. It is brown and slender as my mother's fingers, and I reach for it as I would her hand. I touch it. It is cool, smooth—

Acrid smoke turns my stomach as I watch my father throw yet another painting onto the bonfire behind our house. The curls of my mother's signature go up in flames. A part of me longs to reach through the fire and pull the canvas out, before it is too late, but the greater part of me is rooted to the ground in silent horror. I can only watch, just as I can only watch the memory, as the flames leap higher, devouring paintings of flowers in every color, dazzling bumblebees, brilliant butterflies.

Then I look closer. The flowers are growing from gaping wounds in the rotting remains of what might have once been human. The butterflies' wings are stained red with blood. Bees glut themselves on the nectar of exposed brains.

My father's movements were sluggish with drink, and glass bottles were strewn around the fire, some whole, some broken. What compelled him to clean out my mother's studio now of all times, years after her death, I will never know. I know only that he is thorough, permitting no trace of her to remain.

None, except for the single paintbrush I watched roll from an easel onto the ground, wedging itself between tiles. I tried to paint after the fire, but all I could think of was the paintbrush my mother would never use again, all her paintings lost to flames, and it suddenly seemed pointless. That was the day I gave up sketching leaves and painting flowers. I began pressing and drying plants instead; preserving the dead was the only form of art that interested me anymore. I lost another piece of my mother that day, another piece of myself.

Chapter Sixteen

Muerta's eyes start glowing after she touches a paintbrush, and I know she's having another flashback. This time, though, it fades quickly, and she doesn't need any help from me to come back. I don't know if that's good or bad—if the memory is less powerful, does that mean it won't trigger the orange glow? Or maybe it just means that the memory isn't as traumatic.

When the flashback fades, Muerta looks down at her semitransparent hands and frowns. "I don't feel any different," she says hesitantly. "Does that mean it didn't work?" I can sense her real question just below the surface: does that mean we're trapped here?

I shake my head, refusing to believe it, and I tap my foot, thinking. "Last time, the orange light only came after we *both* had a flashback," I point out, "so maybe I need to remember something, too."

Just as I come to that conclusion, the room around us shifts. Furniture materializes—a desk holding a chunky computer, a pale brown couch with torn cushions, a round, dark brown rug speckled with small white hairs. My dad's office. I remember helping him haul the desk upstairs, and I feel a pang in my chest.

A part of me can't help but wonder if I'll ever see him again. Despite the many, many, *many* reasons my dad and I don't get along, the idea of never seeing him again makes me feel…not quite guilty, but regretful, in a way. As terrible as our relationship can be, there's always been a chance it could get better—a chance I'll lose forever if I turn into an olvidado. I clench my twitching hands into fists. I'm going to live, and, when I'm home, I'm going to fight to make things different.

I drag my hands over the computer keyboard, making sure I touch every key, then I run my fingertips across the screen, leaving faint streaks in the dust that covers it. While I have plenty of memories of using this computer—playing Tetris instead of typing up homework assignments, sneaking in midnight IM sessions with my friends, watching slam poetry performances on YouTube—none of them strike me as particularly important. Not like the flashback I had downstairs.

But I keep trying. I touch the couch, the rug, and even the splintery bookshelves that line the walls. They came with the house, so it's pretty unlikely I'll have any memories attached to them, but still. I glance toward the door. My room is just across the hall, and I'm sure there's something in there that could trigger a flashback, but, if Pablo's continued wailing is any sign, it's still full of olvidados. I tiptoe up to the doorway and risk a peek down the hall. The door to Maria Elena's room is slightly open. I grit my teeth.

"Follow me," I whisper to Muerta, jerking my head toward the hall.

"Is it safe?" Muerta whispers back, eyes wide, clutching the doorway as if it's the only thing keeping her upright.

I'm already halfway across the hall. "Probably not. Come on."

I hear a sound that might be the wind but could also be Muerta sighing. She follows.

The first thing I do is sprint toward the bed and fling myself on it. It's so soft and springy, I bounce a foot into the air before flopping back down. When I was a really little kid, before Maria Elena started doing pageants, back when we actually kind of liked each other, that was how I always entered her room. She would scold me and smooth down the blankets, but, whenever she went into my room, she'd do the exact same thing.

Muerta trails behind me as I drag my hands down the length of Maria Elena's curtains, the puzzles tacked to the wall, the clothes in her closet. I remember ducking behind the curtains during games of hide and seek. More than that, I remember our last conversation.

My chest aches. Threatening tears sting my eyes.

Mom's dead. Mom's dead, Dad's…Dad, and Maria Elena was almost always nice to me in her own way, and how did I repay her? By taking out my anger on her. By implying that she didn't love Mom as much as I did. By doing everything I could to shut her out when she tried her best to be let in.

I sink down onto the round, plush maroon rug at the foot of Maria Elena's bed. I used to lay spread out on this carpet when Dad took Maria Elena to pageants and daydream that the two of us had switched places, that she was the forgotten younger sibling and I was the beautiful, beloved older sister. It never occurred to me to dream of a way we could both be happy. I close my eyes, willing the memories to wash over me, but nothing happens.

I stand up with a sigh, shaking my head. "No luck."

"You have something on your back," says Muerta. "Here, let me—" She pulls a long white strand off my shirt. I recognize it immediately.

"That's from my bow," I reply, recalling how I used to stand on the rug while practicing. "Whenever Maria Elena was out, I played violin in her room because the acoustics were better—she had a higher ceiling."

Hope sparks in Muerta's eyes, and she holds the bow hair toward me. "Do you think—?"

My fingers close around the hair, and a memory surges over me.

I'm standing in the center of the maroon rug, which is in the middle of the room instead of tucked halfway under Maria Elena's bed, and I'm clutching a bow in one trembling hand, the neck of my half-size violin in the other. My shoulders shake, too, spasming and making it all but impossible to maintain the correct posture. Even so, I force myself to drag the bow across the strings, drawing out a sharp, wavering note, the first in a scale. Slowly, I play ascending notes, but the twitching gets worse and worse, until, finally, I fling the bow to the ground in frustration and drop to the ground, burying my face in my hands.

Hot tears pour down my face. My involuntary movements were getting worse and worse, interfering with everything I cared about. Even though I had been taking violin lessons since I was seven, at age ten, even a simple scale was too hard for me, and it would probably only get worse.

"Quiet down," my dad barks from the doorway. "I can't hear the TV." He narrows his eyes. "And get out of your sister's room. You wouldn't like it if she went into your room when *you* weren't around."

Since I knew Maria Elena was at the mall with friends and wouldn't be back for hours, I knew the chances of getting caught were low. As for quieting down: "Don't worry about the noise," I say, holding up my twitching hands. "I can't play anymore."

"That's too bad," says dad with genuine sympathy. Then, before I can even register his unexpected kindness, he adds, "Of course, music was never really your thing, anyway. One artist is enough for any family."

I don't have to ask who he's talking about. I stare down at Maria Elena's immaculately polished guitar, seeing my reflection in its shine. That was the last time I ever played violin.

"Viva? Viva!"

Muerta's voice drags me back to the present. I blink rapidly. "Well, that was definitely a flashback."

"I could tell—your eyes were glowing," says Muerta. "And they glowed earlier, too, after you touched that stain on the couch."

I study my hands, but they don't seem any more solid than before, and there's no trace of orange light. "I don't feel any different, though."

Muerta's lips draw together in worry. "Neither do I."

"Then what—"

"Francisca," a soft, familiar voice interrupts from the doorway. "There you are."

I stiffen, and my jittering fingers move to my throat, where the hand of sand tried to strangle me earlier. "Mom."

"Francisca, please, come with me," my mother pleads. I don't turn to look, but I can almost feel her voice like a warm, physical presence gently winding itself around me. "I just want to protect you."

My shoulders start to shake, just like they did in the memory. "You tried to kill me earlier!"

"That wasn't me!" Desperation floods my mother's voice, and I can't help but turn to look. Her face is just as beautiful as I remembered, even though it's twisted in anguish. "Francisca, I would *never* hurt you. That other ghost is just impersonating me—*I'm* your mother. Please, believe me."

I take a hesitant step toward her. "Mom—" I stop, shaking my head. She's saying all the right things, everything I want to believe. But… "How do I know you're telling the truth?" I force myself to ask, the words bitter on my tongue.

Tears flood my mother's crystalline eyes. "How can you say that?" she whispers, crushed. "All I want to do is protect you. That's why I send Pablo upstairs after you—to watch over you." She moves toward me. "You're in danger, Francisca, but, if you come with me, I can keep you safe." She holds out a pale hand. "Come with me. I can take you away from here, from all these ghosts and memories—"

A shiver runs down my spine. "Memories?"

"All these awful, unhappy memories, yes," says my mother eagerly, nodding. "I can keep you safe—"

"But they're mine," I say.

Mom tilts her head to the side in confusion, and golden hair spills over her shoulder.

"Why don't you want me to regain my memories?" I demand, my voice growing stronger. "They might not be happy, but they're real." I stare my mother in the face; she gazes back through tears. Although it breaks my heart to say it, I add, "That's more than I can say about you."

"Francisca…"

My mother never called me Francisca. She never knew me as Francisca. As much as I would've wanted that to be the case, it just wasn't. I clench my hands into fists. "I don't know who you are, but you are *not* my mother," I say as firmly as I can. No matter how badly I wish she was.

I turn away as my not-mom's sobs grow fainter, then cease.

"She's gone now," says Muerta softly.

I shake my head. Somehow, I don't think we've seen the last of her just yet.

"Wait! I'm not done singing!" cries a desperate voice from across the hall. A ghostly wail, quiet at first, roars louder and louder as my bedroom door trembles on its hinges.

"The olvidados!" Muerta gasps.

Then the door breaks down, unleashing chaos.

Chapter Seventeen

The bedroom door breaks, splinters flying in all directions. A tornado of dust tears across the hallway, faces flickering across its surface before blending back into the spiraling waves of sand. Pablo Flores-Fuentes chases after it, bellowing away and squeezing his accordion, but it ignores him. Partly formed olvidados stumble toward us, trailing grains of sand. Where their faces should be, there are only mouths hanging open. They scream.

Earlier, we were able to scare them away with the orange light, but, even though Viva and I have both been drawn into memories, nothing is happening. I back away from the advancing cyclone of sand until my back is pressed against crushed velvet curtains. Viva doesn't move.

"Viva!" I call out to her.

Viva squares her shoulders. "I think we have to stand up to them!" Her voice sounds thin and strained over the roaring wind. "Last time, we didn't start glowing until after I started fighting that ghost-mom. Maybe if we just stand our ground—"

Maybe is not very comforting. *Maybe* will not protect us from the advancing, writhing dead. Maybe nothing will.

No. I clutch my mother's paintbrush tighter. I won't give in. If Viva is willing to keep fighting, so am I. Still, I can't help but think she's wrong about the orange light. It has to be connected to the memories…but how?

Why are some memories so much stronger than others? Why, when I stood in the room that was once my mother's studio, was the only thing I could remember that last awful day, the day of the fire, the day I stopped painting?

The day I stopped painting.

The strongest memory was about something I lost—my creativity—just like the flashback I had downstairs was of the day I lost my courage. Maybe Viva and I are not only recollecting memories but parts of ourselves. Maybe the real reason we're in la tierra de los olvidados is because we've forgotten who we are, and we can only return to our rightful places once we remember.

Viva is right—the orange light *did* appear when we started fighting back, but perhaps that was less about the action itself than what it represented: reclaiming our bravery. I stare down at my mother's paintbrush and think about what I lost the day my father burned the paintings.

Frantically, I start moving the paintbrush and imagine it leaving thick trails of color in its wake, painting the air. "Viva, I think we have to do something creative!"

Viva half turns. "What?!"

I can't tell if Viva is incredulous at the suggestion, or if she genuinely can't hear me over the advancing wind, so I repeat myself. "Creativity! The memories are trying to tell us about parts of ourselves that we've lost! My memory was about how I stopped painting—"

"—and mine was about how I stopped playing violin!" Viva cries. "You might be—" She shrieks as an olvidado latches onto her ankle. "What do I do? What do I do?"

"Play violin?" I suggest, waving the paintbrush wildly as wind tosses my braid.

Viva kicks an olvidado in the head, and it falls apart in clumps. Another takes its place, moaning and gripping her legs. She shudders. "I don't know if you've noticed, but I don't exactly have a violin on me right now."

"Then pretend!" I yell, tracing the paintbrush in the shape of a flower. "That's what I'm doing!"

"Uh, I'd rather not spend my last seconds of un-life making a total fool of mysel—" Viva's words are cut off by a shriek as long, narrow hands begin reaching out from the tornado, grabbing her hair, her shoulders, her legs, pulling her closer.

"Viva!" I shout. Our only hope is the orange light; Viva *has* to do something creative, and fast. But what? With the olvidados gripping her arms, she can't even pretend to play violin. Her mouth is open, screaming, but, if I couldn't hear, it would almost look like she's singing.

Singing! On the day she moved in, when she first decorated her room, Viva was singing. How did that song go? I can only remember the very beginning. I think it went something like…

"*Fran-cis-ca!*" I sing at the top of my lungs.

At the sound of those three notes, Viva seems to stand straighter. She turns to me—as much as she can, with the olvidados tugging on her arms, pulling her deeper into the tornado—and something like hope sparks in her eyes.

I sing again. "*Fran-cis-ca!*" I gesture wildly for her to continue the melody, then go back to painting the air.

Viva's voice is barely audible over the wind, but what I can make out sounds like: "*Quieres llevar montañas por mano…*"

I notice orange light pouring from the tip of my paintbrush. My hand is glowing, too, the radiance making its way down my arms. "It's working! Keep singing!"

"*Quieres cuentar las estrellas solá!*" Viva sings, her voice growing more confident as the olvidados shriek, shrinking back. "*Solá,*" she echoes, looking down at her hands, encased in brilliant orange light. The hands that seized her arms crumble to dust, and she lifts her left hand so the wrist is pointed upward, the right hand curved over midair as if she's holding something invisible. Then she makes a sawing motion, and I realize she's pretending to play violin.

I paint with bolder strokes, imagining splatters of orange filling the sky. The glow expands, trailing down my arm to my chest, then spreading up my neck, then down my stomach and legs, until a sense of warm lightness fills my entire body. My feet lift off the ground, and, laughing from sheer joy, I float over to Viva.

To my surprise, Viva grins and grabs my hand, pulling me to earth with a twirl.

"*Francisca,*" she sings, leading me in a dance as the orange light passes from my hands to hers. "*Tus amigas siempre estarán contigo! Nunca tienes que sentirte solá.*"

"*Solá,*" I chime in, remembering.

"Yeah!" Viva laughs. "You've got it!"

We spin, we romp, we glide, and, all the while, we glow. We sing at the top of our lungs and dance until we can barely stand upright, and the tornado of sand dissolves into clouds of harmless dust, faces and limbs crumbling in on themselves into piles of dirt on the ground. I pull Viva into the air with me for one final twirl, then we lightly return to the ground as our orange light fades to the final strains of her song.

Chapter Eighteen

As soon as my feet touch the ground, I turn to Muerta. "We need to find more memories before the olvidados come back."

Muerta nods, then pales. "There!" she cries, pointing with her paintbrush. "There's one coming toward us!"

Sure enough, there's a figure of sand on its hands and knees, crawling across the hall.

"Wait!" it shouts with a familiar voice. "It's just me!"

I lower my fists; Muerta lowers the paintbrush. "Pablo," we say at the same time, relieved.

At the sound of his name, Pablo smiles. I can tell that he's smiling because he actually has a face now—eyes, nose, lips, and all. In the moment before his features fade back into dust, I try to see if I can spot any hint of myself in there. After all, we're technically related. His eyes are almond-shaped, more like Muerta's than mine, but he has a wider nose than she does, closer to my dad's. Then an uneasy feeling settles in my stomach. It's not the first time Pablo's shown his face, but it's the first time I've really looked at it—the first time I recognized that he's a person, like me.

Or, at least, he used to be, before he was forgotten.

I extend a hand to help him up. A tentacle-like limb extends upward, coalescing into a hand that grips mine, pulling Pablo to his feet.

"Thank you for distracting the olvidados earlier," says Muerta. "We wouldn't have been able to unlock those memories without you."

I nod, then put a hand on my hip. I can feel grains of sand lodged under my fingernails. "How did my mom—" I wince, then correct myself "—the ghost *pretending* to be Mom convince you to start helping us?"

Pablo tilts his head in confusion. "How did who convince me to what?" He shakes his head, stirring up a cloud of dust. "I decided to help because you girls helped *me*. Or, at least, she did," he adds, pointing at Muerta before turning back toward me. "*You* were telling her to close the door."

I scratch my head. "Yeah, sorry about that."

"Besides," he says, his voice softening. "I think you two are on the right track, unlocking memories and all that. You give me hope." A faint smile flickers across his face before his features are obscured. "Maybe I won't end up a complete olvidado after all. Maybe, if I start collecting memories of my own, I'll be able to pass on, too."

I can't help but grimace at his word choice. *Passing on* might be better than becoming an olvidado, but I have no intention of dying.

Pablo's accordion spreads out between his hands. "I saw you two singing and dancing earlier. Mind if I join in?"

Muerta and I share a glance of trepidation. Then Muerta manages a weak smile. "Yes, of course."

I brace myself for the first horrifying screech, but it never comes. Instead, a tumble of perfectly passable notes pours from the accordion, and Pablo sings the folk tune from earlier in a thoroughly average voice.

"That's...not bad," I say.

Muerta nods vigorously, the sunflower in her hair flapping. "Yes, it's not awful at all!"

For a split second, Pablo's face returns, flashing a bittersweet smile at our measured praise. "But it's not good, is it?" His face sinks in on itself. "It's forgettable, just like I am."

"Don't say that," says Muerta in a hush, looking concerned.

"Hey, you saved us," I add, kneeling so my face is level with where his would be, if he still had one. "I'll always remember you for that."

Slowly, almost shyly, eyes materialize, followed by a half-smiling mouth and a nose that looks like mine.

"You know, I used to play my accordion badly on purpose," he confides in us. "I'd sit outside in front of the house and play as loud as I could, so everyone would hear it." He sighs. "I knew I wasn't talented enough to hold anyone's attention, but, I thought, maybe if I was bad enough…"

"You thought it would make people remember you," says Muerta in a soft voice.

Pablo nods, closing his eyes. Sand buries them. "As you can see, it didn't work."

"I guess it didn't," I say, a feeling I can't quite name stirring in my chest. Pity, maybe?

No—it's recognition.

I swallow. In my own way, I've been doing exactly what Pablo Flores did: trying to make my mark by being loud and abrasive, unforgettable for all the wrong reasons. I knew I'd never be a good girl, like Maria Elena, so I took myself out of the competition. Rude, quick-tempered, sarcastic—that's who I was, but was it really who I wanted to be?

When did I start using anger as armor? When did I forget how to be kind?

"Muerta," I say, turning and taking her hand. "I'm sorry." I let out a deep breath. "I've been going through a lot, and obviously all this—" I wave my hand "—haunting and being dead stuff isn't making it any easier, but it's not fair for me to take that out on you." I meet her eyes, and, for the first time, I register what a pretty shade of light brown they are. "You're just as lost as I am, but you've been looking out for me this whole time. I don't know what I'd do without you."

Muerta smiles and gives my hand a gentle squeeze before letting go. "I forgive you, Viva."

I smile back. "Thanks."

Pablo clumsily slaps me on the shoulder with a handless arm. It feels like getting hit by a sock full of sand. "And *I* forgive *you* for telling her to close the door on me earlier."

I nod. "Glad to hear it."

"But, now, I must be going," says Pablo. "You girls have inspired me to start looking for memories of my own." A wistful note enters his voice, and a pair of longing eyes gaze out from his dusty, weathered face. "My wife used to love the oleander bush out back. I've tried not to think about Graciela because it hurts so much, but I think it's time."

Muerta tilts her head up to meet his eyes. "Pablo Flores-Fuentes, we'll meet again soon in la Tierra de los Muertos."

"No offense, but once I get out of here, I hope I don't see either of y'all for a long, long time," I say, making Muerta and Pablo laugh. I nod at Pablo. "Seriously, though, good luck."

Pablo pantomimes tipping his hat to Muerta and I and leaves the room. I can hear his footsteps on the stairs, then I hear nothing at all.

Muerta gazes into the distance. "I wonder what they have forgotten."

I shift my weight uncomfortably. I know exactly what *they* she's talking about, and I don't like it. I've come around on Pablo, but the other olvidados—those horrible sand monsters—I don't want to admit that they were ever anything like me.

"We've all got something, I guess," I say with a shrug.

"Like Abril," says Muerta softly. "She forgot how to speak. I hope she was never here." She sighs, lowering her head. "But I can imagine it all too well."

"I think Abril's fine," I tell her. "Her family's still around, you know."

Muerta lifts her face. "The San Miguels?"

I nod. "They run the library, and they're just crazy about this town and its history. If anyone's got a shot at being remembered around here, it's their relatives."

"Does being remembered by others matter if we forget ourselves?" Muerta asks, and there's no answer.

"I guess it depends what counts as forgetting," I say at last. "I mean, everything in town seems like it's been forgotten in one way or another. There's that park that used to be a river, the old train station no one uses, that statue—"

"The statue of Claudia at the border of the town?" Muerta asks.

"It's not at the border of anything anymore. It's by the library," I explain. "And the statue's been torn apart. The top part is missing—all you can see is the foundation and a plaque that says 'Claudia' on it."

Muerta looks mournful. "It's terrible to think that even Claudia has been forgotten."

She says it like Claudia's some kind of hero. I feel a little ashamed for not caring when the San Miguels tried to tell me about the town's history. To be fair, I did have other things on my plate. Still, to make up for it in some small way, I ask, "Did you know her?"

"No," says Muerta. "She died in 1812."

"The year the town was founded," I recall.

"Oh, it had been around before then," Muerta replies, "but that is when it was officially recognized as a town, I suppose. Before that, it was a refuge for runaways. Slaves from the haciendas, indigenous families like my mother's who were forced to flee from Spaniards—Claudia created a haven here, and she led others toward it."

"And now no one remembers her," I finish. No thanks to people like me. I turn to Muerta. "You said the boundaries between life and death were weak around the house because of you. How do you know that?"

"I don't," Muerta admits, "but it's what I believe."

"If forgetting is what makes the difference, maybe the whole town has weak barriers because no one remembers Claudia anymore," I suggest. "In a way, the town forgot about itself, and now Claudesville is like its own little Land of the Forgotten."

"We remembered Claudia in my time," says Muerta.

"Maybe there was something else you were forgetting back then."

Muerta is still for a moment, then she whispers, "Our language." In a stronger voice, she adds, "When they took us to school, we were only allowed to speak English. We would come back home and have a hard time breaking the habit." Tears well up in her eyes. "There were times during my last conversations with my grandfather that I struggled to understand what he was saying, I was so out of practice. Some of the younger parents started speaking English with their children right away, and they never learned Spanish at all."

"I only know a few words," I confess. Mostly curse words, but I don't tell her that.

Muerta sighs, and I feel bad, then annoyed with myself for feeling bad. What was I supposed to do—raise myself to speak Spanish? If anything, it's my dad's fault for not bothering, but I guess he couldn't teach me what he didn't know. He barely spoke Spanish either. I guess my grandparents were like the younger parents in Muerta's village, the ones that figured it was easier to start the kids off with English right off the bat. So maybe it's no one's fault, or else it's the fault of so many people spread out across such a stupidly long amount of time that it's pointless to try and piece it together.

"It wasn't only Spanish," Muerta continued. "My mother's people had their own language, and so did many of the others who came to

Claudia, but they were forgotten, too, or stolen."

"Plenty of forgetting to go around, I guess." My words are hollow, but I'm slowly filled with determination.

It doesn't have to stay like this. When I get back to the Land of the Living, I can carry these memories forward. I can learn about this place from the San Miguels and the library. I can study Spanish and the languages that came before. I can make sure no one forgets that, yes, terrible things happened in the Flores house, but there was a girl that lived there once, and her name was Francisca, and she was brave and kind. And a friend.

Chapter Nineteen

I peer cautiously down the hall, which seems to be free of olvidados. "You wanted to look through the bedroom earlier," I say to Viva. "It seems safe, for now."

"Sounds good," Viva replies, entering the hall. As she leads the way, I continue to scan for olvidados, so I'm caught off-guard by a sudden crunch. "Ow!" Viva cries, hopping on one leg. I look down and see soil, fragments of clay, and crushed yellow flowers. "Why is there a flower pot in the middle of the hallway?"

"Remember how the olvidados threw all my stuff around?" I say. "We must be in my house now."

Viva huffs, stepping aside gingerly and gesturing for me to lead. "Guess it's your turn, then."

"It *does* seem like we're taking turns," I say slowly. "So far, the memories have alternated—one for me, one for you. I wonder why. Do you think it could be because we came here together?"

Viva shakes her head. "You and your 'why's."

We've reached the bedroom door; in Viva's time, it was torn off its hinges by olvidados, but, here, it is only slightly ajar. "I don't understand why you aren't more curious about all of this," I say, opening the door.

"It's not that I don't want answers," says Viva, walking into the bedroom. "I just want to get out of here more." She picks one of my old sketchbooks off the floor and tosses it to me. "This do anything for you?"

The sketchbook has a fine brown leather cover embroidered with yellow flowers along the edges—my mother's handiwork. I can recall the day she gave it to me, the hours I spent doodling flowers and leaves inside, how I set it on my desk the night of my suicide to run my fingers over the flowers on the cover one last time, but none of the memories grip me.

I sigh, letting the sketchbook drop to my side as I survey the room. There's a hole in the window from where my music box was thrown out, and my curtains are wadded up on the floor, the rod hanging at an awkward angle. Loose papers litter the floor along with more smashed flower pots—Viva minces toward my bed, careful to avoid stepping on them—and the grout between tiles is caked with dust. I shudder at the thought of it forming into olvidados.

Viva drops to her knees and tilts her head to the side, studying the space beneath my bed. "There's a bunch of stuff under here," she reports. "Come check it out."

I wend my way across the room and kneel beside Viva, who is now laying on the ground, her arm outstretched. "There's something lumpy here in the back," she mutters. "Wadded-up cloth or something."

"Don't touch it!" I panic, hyperventilating when I don't even need to breathe. "Just—just leave that alone," I gasp.

Viva raises an eyebrow. "Why?"

I force a smile. "You and your 'why's.'"

"If you don't want to touch it, that probably means you need to," Viva points out, sitting up and crossing her arms.

I shake my head. I know what it is, and I know exactly what I'll remember if I do.

Viva stares me down for a moment, then lunges under the bed. I jump back, throwing my hands over my eyes. It doesn't matter. I see it all too clearly in my mind: the lumpy oval of its body, the flap of brown fabric meant to represent long, flowing hair, the red skirt Maria Elena stitched into place herself.

Isabela: my old ragdoll. She was only a little smaller than an actual newborn, and I used to cradle her to my chest in an imitation of one of my mother's gestures. For a moment, I wonder how I could have picked that up from my mother when I was the youngest. Perhaps I only saw her carrying bundles of clothes. It is easier to think of my mother and the mystery in her arms than Isabela herself. She was once my prized possession, but, now, even the thought of her turns my stomach.

"Viva, please," I whisper, though what I'm asking her for, I'm not sure.

I'm expecting her to thrust the doll at me, forcing me into the memory, but she doesn't. "Whatever happened—it's just a memory now," says Viva gently. "Just let it play out. I'll be right here next to you the whole time. *Francisca,*" she sings, half-smiling. "*Nunca tienes que sentirte solá.*"

"*Solá,*" I breathe, meeting Viva's dark, daring eyes. I inhale deeply, then reach for the doll.

"Got it!" Maria Elena's laughing voice rings out several feet above my head. She's perched in a crook between tree branches, waving my ragdoll in the air triumphantly. "Throw it higher next time," she adds, tossing it down to me as I lean out my bedroom window to catch it. "Climbing this high isn't even a challenge anymore."

Down below, Abril and Maya jump up and down, cheering my sister on. "Higher, higher!" they chant. Even a story up, I can still tell them apart because Maya stands closer to the tree, almost directly under Maria Elena, and keeps glancing up in awe. Sunset slants across Abril's hair; Maya is darkened by the shadow of the tree.

I giggle and rear back my arm, throwing as high as I can. The ragdoll flies in a high, assured arc, lodging between a fork in one of the highest branches of the orange tree.

"Child's play!" Maria Elena declares, grinning. She picks her way up the increasingly slender branches, moving with natural, careless grace in spite of the way her long hair and skirt keep getting snarled by twigs. At fourteen, especially with our mother gone, Maria Elena is expected to be the woman of the house, yet, somehow, no matter how many responsibilities are heaped upon her shoulders, she always makes time for fun. I know, despite her teasing, that she loves this game as much as I do.

Maria Elena climbs higher, higher. She reaches for the doll, enclosing it in her fist. She holds it up with a whoop of triumph, silhouetted against the sun. Her cheer is so loud, it almost camouflages the sound of snapping wood. Almost.

"The branch—" I cry, reaching out the window as if one of my small hands could stop her fall.

It takes less than a second for Maria Elena's cheer to become a scream, but that second is the longest of my life. I see her long, curly brown hair whipping in the wind, her torn skirt billowing outward as if to cushion her, her thin, calloused hands desperately searching for anything to latch onto, finding nothing but air. For a moment, the sunlight brightens her eyes, turning them the most beautiful, luminous amber I've ever seen. Then she hits the ground. Her eyes close. She is silent.

There's still screaming, of course: mine, Abril's, Maya's. Especially Maya. The branch that broke beneath Maria Elena's weight scratched her badly, and she is bleeding in several places. I do not know this at the time, but those scratches will soon become infected, and, in less than a week, Abril San Miguel, one of *los dos*, the inseparable two, will become Abril the silent, and Maya will be dead. Like my sister. Muerta, both of them.

Muerta, muerta, muerta...

"Muerta, Muerta!"

I notice a distant pressure on my shoulders.

"Muerta, you're having a flashback," says a loud, clear voice. "Can you hear me?" Warm, rough hands grab mine. "Squeeze back if you can hear me."

I manage a faint squeeze. Slowly, I recognize the voice—Viva's—and I recognize my room as it is now, destroyed by olvidados, not the way it looked the day my sister died so many, many years ago.

Tears well up in my eyes, and I let the ragdoll drop to the ground. After what happened to Maria Elena, I couldn't bear to look at it again, but getting rid of it felt just as wrong. I compromised with myself, hiding it under my bed, so I would always know where it was but never have to see it.

A broken whisper escapes my lips. "Maria Elena, I'm sorry." My cheeks are hot with tears. "We don't have to play anymore. Never again, never again. I'm sorry..."

Viva stiffens at the sound of my sister's name but does not comment. Instead, she holds her arms out, and I walk into them. Her embrace is clumsy, like it's been a while since she's given one, but she holds me tight enough that I can feel it even in the near-intangible, ghostly state my body is in.

"If you want to talk about it, I'll listen," Viva offers.

So, I tell her, and she holds me.

"I always blamed myself," I choke out. "It was my game—my doll—my fault—"

Viva shakes her head. "No, it wasn't. It was an accident—that's not anyone's fault."

My cheeks are hot with tears. "She wouldn't have been in that tree in the first place if it wasn't for me."

"You're right." Viva speaks so fiercely, it stuns my crying to a standstill. "She *was* in that tree because of you, because she *loved* you." Her neck twitches, but her eyes are firm and sure as they meet mine. "I might not know your sister, but I can tell she really cared about you, and I know she wouldn't want you to blame yourself for what happened."

I let out a deep breath and wipe my eyes. I even manage a faint smile for Viva. "Thank you."

Viva smiles back, but there's a glint of regret in her eyes. "You know, I have a sister. Her name's Maria Elena, too." She sighs, running a hand through her short hair. "We don't really get along. The last time I spoke with her—" She grimaces.

"I know, I was there," I remind her. "As a ghost."

"Right, yeah." Viva looks embarrassed. "So, you know I'm pretty much a failure as a sister, then, huh?"

I take Viva's hand. "You'll speak to her again," I promise. "And, when you do, remember me, and my Maria Elena, and—" my voice quivers like the leaves of the orange tree "—and remember that you won't have your sister forever."

Viva nods. "I'll never forget."

Chapter Twenty

As my familiar furniture manifests around us, I try to distinguish the mess I left behind from the damage caused by olvidados. My bed was already unmade, the blankets wadded up on the ground beside it, but the mattress is shredded, as if it's been raked by claws. The blot of red nail polish on my desk has spread into a stain that drips onto the floor, bleeding into the carpet, but I don't remember ever putting the cap back on, so it might have been that way already. The cardboard boxes I had piled in the corner have been flung all over the place. My violin case is open, and the bow, snapped in half, held together only by its hair, lies several feet away. My pictures are torn from the wall, scattered across the room.

"I'm sorry about your violin," says Muerta softly, picking up the broken bow.

I shrug, then my shoulders twitch. "I can't play it anyway."

"Why not?" she asks.

"It's too small, for one. That, and—" I hold up my hands so she can see my fingers twitching "—I can't hold the bow right, can't keep the posture…" I shrug again. "There's a lot of things I can't do anymore."

"Anymore," Muerta notes. "Did something happen?"

I sigh. Instead of answering, I make my way toward the dollhouse. If Muerta can face the memory of losing her sister, it's about time I face my last memory of mom. When I open the dollhouse, the dolls are all exactly where I left them, except for the one that got beheaded. There's Luna, her mother, and her father, all tied to the elegant pink dining room chairs by double-knotted rainbow yarn.

I reach for the mother doll and stroke her silky blonde hair. Sure enough, a flashback follows.

Smack!

"Don't you touch me!"

I hold up the mother doll, pretending that my mother's high, hysterical voice is coming from her instead. I move her stiff arm so her hand strikes the father doll's face.

Smack!

"Don't you ever touch me again! Damn it, Diego!"

I hold up little Luna and whisper, "Mom, are you okay?"

"I've had it with you, all of you!" the mother doll shrieks. "I could've been somebody, you know? I could've gotten a record deal and everything if *someone* hadn't knocked me up!"

"You still could've had one if *someone* had just gotten the abortion!"

"I was sixteen!" cries the mother doll. "I was scared!"

At eight, I try to imagine being twice my age, all grown up. I think, *mom's so pretty, and she sings so well.* She should have gotten a record deal. She's exactly right. I wonder what an abortion is.

I hear the door slam, and I drop the dolls and race downstairs. I want to find Mom and give her a hug, and tell her that she has the most beautiful voice in the world, that it's okay if she hits Dad sometimes because he almost always hits first, that I love her so much…

Mom stomps across the porch, and I burst out of the door right as she starts getting into her car: a worn-out red minivan.

"Mom!" I shout. "Wait for me!"

Mom loves me more than anything, I tell myself.

With a cold, mask-like face I refuse to acknowledge, my mother slams the car door.

Mom would never leave me.

The engine revs.

She'll come back. She has to come back.

Mom's car pulls out of the driveway, and a part of me must know the truth, because I jump on my bike and tear after her.

"Mom!" I scream, unable to see through a haze of tears. "Mom, don't go!" I'm crying so hard, I'm so focused on Mom, I don't notice our neighbor's car backing out of their garage, and he must not notice me, either. Everything goes black.

I hear Muerta's hushed voice in my ear: "Viva?"

Sighing, I open my eyes. "I'm back."

"I saw flashes," she says; I remember seeing a bit of her memory downstairs, with the black-haired girl and the pressure of the boy's mouth, and I figure the same thing must have happened for her. "Viva, I'm so sorry."

"She never came back, in case you were wondering," I say flatly. My neck twitches. "Dad took me to the hospital, but, aside from a broken leg, they said I was fine. I didn't even have a concussion, somehow." My hands shake. "But, more and more, I couldn't control my hands. My neck and arms were spasming. They said it was just a nervous tic and it would go away, but it hasn't."

I press my eyes shut as tightly as I can, willing myself not to cry. "Every time something twitches, I have to do everything I can to not think of that day. When I can't play violin, when I miss another easy round at a bowling tournament and let the team down, whenever I walk instead of taking my bike—" I suck in a shuddering breath. "It's like my body's broken because my family's broken. I can't separate the two. I can't forget. I tried so hard—"

Muerta touches my shoulder so lightly, it feels like a sunbeam glancing off my arm.

"The first thing I did when I got back from the hospital," I continue staring at the mother doll in my hand, "was tie these dolls to the chairs. I never wanted to play with them again." Finally, the tears come. I sniffle. "I didn't want anyone else to leave."

Muerta doesn't try to tell me that my mom's disappearance had nothing to do with me. She must have seen enough of the memory to know that it isn't true, that what I've been telling myself all this time—she loves me, she misses me, soon she'll come back—is just a desperate lie.

That time with the scarf—it wasn't the first time I thought of suicide. In some ways, it wasn't even the closest. If I'd known how to do it then, the night I got home from the hospital, twitching and shaking, limping in my bulky cast that no one had signed—

I wound up in the laundry room somehow, and the sight of the orange detergent bottle made me cry, because Mom always did the laundry, and she used to tell me not to drink it.

She wasn't there to tell me that night.

I don't know what I expected it to feel like, but it was slippery, and thick, and cloyingly sweet. I choked down a mouthful, but my stomach rebelled. I gagged, coughing, then vomited. Either I didn't swallow enough to begin with, or I threw up too much, but my dad found me the next morning asleep in a puddle of puke, still alive.

He helped me stand up and walked me to the kitchen. He rinsed dried vomit out of my hair in the sink and fixed me a fried bologna sandwich. I ate it with the taste of detergent and stomach acid thick on my tongue. We never talked about that night. There were so many things we never talked about.

After that, I lived in denial. It was the only way I could live. Was that what I lost that day, my will to live?

My gaze shifts from the mother doll to the daughter, Luna. I gave her the name I found more beautiful than any in the world. The same name I gave myself. I remember my first time hearing "Francisca" by Luna del Sol on the Mexican alternative station my Tia Lola listens to at her tattoo parlor and feeling like it had been written just for me. I remember bowling with Cat and Angie at the mall during the summer, no pressure to win, just our overlapping laughter as I dropped the ball during a spasm and bowled a perfect strike. I remember Maria Elena teaching me how to use eyeliner as part of a natural, everyday look—a lesson I largely ignored, preferring to cake on as much as humanly possible, when I wore it at all.

No. I set the mother doll down and pick up Luna. I might have lost my mother that day, but I didn't lose my will to live. Not entirely.

What did I lose, then, and what do I need to find if I want to get out of here?

A low moan builds beneath us, getting louder by the second. The stairs groan with the weight of the dead. The wind howls. Muerta and I share a glance; the olvidados are coming back. Any second now, they'll have us cornered, and Pablo Flores-Fuentes isn't around to distract them a second time.

"Any ideas?" I ask her.

She clutches her old rag doll to her chest, shaking her head, eyes wide. She looks like a scared little girl.

A little girl…

Using my teeth, I tear the yarn binding Luna to the chair and brandish her, moving one arm up and down in a karate-chopping motion. "Hi-yah!" I squeal. "Whoop-pow!"

Muerta looks at me like I've lost my mind. "What are you doing?"

"Both of our memories are about how we stopped playing with

dolls," I say quickly, raising my voice so Muerta can hear me over the wind. "So, maybe, if we play with dolls now—"

"No," Muerta interjects, "that's not what the memories were really about." She gazes down at her rag doll's lopsided button eyes. "They were about grief, and guilt, and—" Her eyes latch onto mine. "I think we have to forgive ourselves." A sudden smile brightens her face. "And what better way to forgive ourselves than by playing with the toys we felt like we didn't deserve anymore? Viva, you're brilliant!"

"Uh-huh," I agree, although, really, my plan was just to play with dolls and hope for the best. Muerta's explanation makes a lot of sense, though.

The door is still in splinters from earlier, so I can see the olvidados dragging themselves up the stairs and down the hall, trailing clouds of dust in their wake. Maybe using the plural is wrong—there's just one writhing, slithering mass with many mouths and empty eye sockets and tentacle-like limbs that end in a sharp point. It digs into the floor, cracking tile, and drags itself forward, moaning in a chorus of voices: men's, women's, children's. There's even a wail that sounds animal, like the cry of a coyote or wolf. It seems more solid than the olvidados that chased us earlier, and, even though Muerta is stunned silent, I can see the questions building in her eyes as she reaches for her sunflower.

Why is it more solid? Does that mean it's stronger? Are we getting weaker? How many more memories do we need to find before we end up like that?

"Luna to the rescue!" I roar, running into the hall.

"Viva!" Muerta shrieks. "Get back here!"

"Pow! Zap! Woosh!" I cry out the first action-y noises I can think of, waving Luna up and down. I make her kick her legs out. "Bam! Boom!" I stare down at my hands hopefully; no trace of orange light. "A little help here, maybe!" I call over my shoulder to Muerta.

"This is ridiculous," says Muerta so quietly I can barely hear her. Then, loudly: "Ooh, Isabela's gonna get you!" She sprints into the hall beside me, flailing her ragdoll so its head lolls round and round. Our eyes meet, and the absurdity of the situation hits us all at once. I snort; she giggles, then we're both screaming, almost crying with laughter, clutching each other and our dolls, sinking to the floor as an orange glow overtakes us both and the olvidados dissolve to dust.

All but one.

Out of the corner of my eye, I see a white hand pick up the mother doll, still tied to her chair. "A fitting image," a familiar voice spits. Cold hands grip the back of my neck, and I'm dragged through the floor into darkness.

Chapter Twenty-One

Viva and the white woman in red melt into a pool of blackness before my eyes, sinking through the gap between tiles and vanishing.

Is this it? Have I lost her? Pressure builds in my chest; tears threaten to overwhelm my eyes. Then I force myself to breathe deeply. Panic won't help me save Viva. I don't know where she is, but it's possible she's still in the house. My eyes dart toward the stairwell; my body follows. I race downward, ignoring the creak of wood beneath my feet, but there's no sign of her in the living room—my living room.

The phonograph lies on its side. Oranges from an upset bowl are everywhere. Glass from shattered picture frames litters the floor, and I have to weave around them to avoid being cut. Then I hear noise from below: cruel laughter, crying. I recognize Viva's voice, pleading. She must be in the basement.

I tear through the living room, the kitchen, until I'm running through the arcades that surround the house, just as I used to run from Abril and Maya. I grab the basement door and pull as hard as I can. At first, it refuses to budge, but I manage to yank it open, exposing a thin, wooden ladder that leads into utter darkness.

Wind whispers around me, running its hot fingers through my hair, and clouds of dust murmur as they try to coalesce into hands around my ankles. I stare up at the unending gray sky; a bright round spot, either the sun or a full moon, peers through the gloom like an eye. For a moment, I see myself as the eye would: as a tiny, trembling, insignificant insect. Then I hear Viva screaming below, and I launch down the ladder. Cobwebs collect around my feet as splinters slice into my hands, but I refuse to acknowledge the pain. Viva is still shouting; Viva still needs me.

The only light in the basement comes from the door I've left open—a pale gloom. Light seems drawn to Viva's mother's hair, making it appear white rather than blonde. Her back is to me as she lifts Viva by the throat. Viva's eyes widen as she notices me, but I quickly hold a finger to my lips. Her mother's ghost is more powerful than I am; if Viva and I are to have any chance at getting away from her, it's essential that I maintain the element of surprise.

"Finally, you'll understand what you did to me," Viva's mother hisses. Viva chokes out another cry, but she can't speak. Her mother smacks her across the face. "Shut up!" she shrieks. "You, and your sister, and your bastard father—you took everything from me, but now—" a wild laugh tears from her throat "—now *I'm* in control." Another smack. "You ruined my life, but now, in death…" Her voice drops to a harsh whisper, one I can barely hear over the wind above. "I'm going to ruin you."

I stand in Viva's mother's shadow, desperately trying to think of a plan, but there's nothing I can do. Even our one method of frightening olvidados away—the orange light—didn't seem to have any effect on her upstairs, and I can't think of any particularly strong memories attached to this basement. When my mother was alive, we used it to store fruits and vegetables for the winter; when she died, the door was locked, everything beneath it left to rot. The sickly-sweet stench of decay is heavy in the air even now.

My fingers reach for my sunflower, but I can no longer feel it. I need to act, but all that comes to mind are questions. Why is this ghost so much stronger than the other olvidados? Is it because her death is the most recent? Does she have more memories intact? Why is she haunting Viva? I run a hand down the length of my braid, choking back a sob, collapsing in on myself. Why is any of this happening? Why did I ever think I could help? Who do I think I am?

Before my eyes, my fingers start to crumble to dust. I scream, then clap what remains of my hands over my mouth. It's too late.

Viva's mother whips around. She sneers. "Well, look at that, —" She calls Viva by a name I don't recognize, a boy's name, one that brings tears to her eyes. "Your friend came to rescue you. Isn't that sweet?"

"Put her down!" I try to sound commanding, but my voice is high and thin. My hands shake, and grains of sand fall away faster and faster. I clench them into fists to try to hold them together, but Viva's mother takes this as a sign of aggression and laughs.

"You want to fight me, little girl?"

"I—I will if I have to!" I stammer, standing my ground even as I tremble, even as sand from what were once my fingers collects in my palms.

Viva's mother steps forward, and light slants over her head, illuminating the curved flank of the cistern behind her.

The cistern—

An ache builds behind my forehead, as if ghosts are drumming on my skull. My eyes can't leave the cistern; my body is drawn toward it. I'm not having any memories, at least not yet, but…

I dodge Viva's mother and launch myself forward, sliding on my stomach toward the cistern. Rough stone snags at my blouse and bruises my legs, but in seconds, what remains of my hand is pressed firmly against cool metal, and a flashback begins.

"Hide," my father whispers urgently, pushing my head down so I am hidden behind the cistern. Pipes branch overhead, rattling and moaning, and the sound of water rushing through them makes me think of sobbing ghosts, and a plaintive cry leaves my throat. "Sh-sh," my father soothes. "Just be quiet. Everything will be—"

"Where is she?" my mother's wild shriek reverberates off the stone walls and seems to make the pipes shiver. My mother wails. "Francisca, Francisca, where are you?"

I open my mouth to tell her, to say whatever it takes to make my mother stop crying, but my father raises his voice before I can speak. "Elena, you need to calm down," he says in a loud but measured, cautious voice.

"Calm down?" My mother's words are choked by sobs. "Ana is dead!" Her voice breaks. "Our baby, our little girl—"

The words seem to come from far away, obscured by distance. Then they are deafening, pressingly close.

Ana. Dead.

Ana…

Ana Flores, my younger sister.

I remember leaning over Ana's crib, holding Isabela within reach of her baby fists, only to be rushed out of the nursery by mother.

"Ana's sick," she whispers. "That grimy thing is only going to make it worse."

I remember trying to sneak Ana a spoonful of squash, my least favorite vegetable, at the dinner table when my mother had her back turned only to get caught. My mother's eyes widened as if I was giving my sister rat poison.

"Are you trying to choke her?" she hisses.

"Elena!" my father rumbled from the head of the table.

My mother shrank back into her seat, muttering to herself as she stroked Ana's scant hair. Maria Elena shot me a sympathetic look across the table, then made a face, making me smile.

I remember holding Isabela tightly, the way I saw my mother holding Ana.

I remember the day Ana was born. Maria Elena and I were in the sunflower field with Abuelo Francisco when Abril and Maya's older brother came running from the village, scattering the little brown birds pecking at seeds at our feet.

"It's Señora Flores," he panted, red in the face. "She's bleeding a lot, and the baby—something's wrong with the baby, too—"

My mother *did* stop painting in the year before her death. My mother *was* sick. But that was not all that happened.

I had a little sister, and she was sick as well. So sick that, at first, my mother thought it was safer if no one saw the baby at all. So sick that the rumor spread that the baby died, and my mother liked it that way, because it meant no one would ever try to take Ana from her, the way they took Maria Elena, and me, and the other children away at the end of each summer.

"Where is Francisca?" The urgency in my mother's voice is almost enough to make me come out from behind the cistern, but light from above glances off the knife in my mother's hand. I do not move. "We'll all go together," says my mother in a horrible, breathless rush. "Ana won't have to be alone. Ana, my baby, in la Tierra de los Muertos—"

"Elena, you need to—" My father cries out, and it is only when I hear the sound of the knife being pulled from his flesh that I realize what has happened.

"Papí!" I cry, leaping out from behind the cistern.

My mother's eyes widen. She lunges with the knife—

My father tears the blade from her hand and drives it through her chest. My mother gasps and sinks to the floor. My father, breathing heavily, falls with her, clutching his left shoulder where her knife broke the skin.

I return to the present, and tears fill my eyes. For more than half my life, I hated my father for killing my mother, but he had only done it to protect himself.

To protect me.

I am so stunned by the realization, I make no move to pull away when a hand of sand forms around my ankles, followed by an arm, a shoulder, a neck, a head. A face.

For a moment, I see my father's face, and I see mine: my lips and Maria Elena's, eyes the same light brown as mine. He even has the moles I share with Abuelo Francisco, almost but not quite concealed by the wiry stubble on his cheeks. Then the face starts sinking into itself, and the gaping mouth lets out a low moan. I realize he's trying to speak to me.

"Hide," he murmurs, his voice fading into the soft sound of cascading sand as his mouth falls shut. With a pang in my chest, I recognize him as the olvidado that lifted me when I fell outside, when I first tried and failed to protect Viva. Even with the memory of his own face lost, with only the barest semblance of a self left beneath the shifting sand, my father recognized me, and tried his best to help.

Even when I hated him, my father loved me. He loves me even now.

I drop to my knees and take what remains of his face in my hands, kissing his forehead. Flecks of hot dust coat the back of my throat, making me gag, but I don't pull back. I place my hands where his cheeks should be, and it is as if my touch sculpts them into being. Stubble prickles my palms; eyelashes tickle the underside of my throat, hands reach up to take mine.

"Papí," I whisper. "I remember you."

Brilliant orange light encases my father's body. Sand builds upon sand, thickening into solid limbs, a body, a fixed face. He stands, his hands still grasping mine, and my fingers reform at his touch.

"Francisca!" my father gasps.

"Papí!" Tears of joy surge down my cheeks. I hold him tightly. I never want to let go again.

"I died not long after I lost you," he whispers. Guilt clenches my heart. I was the only family he had left, and I chose—I *chose*—to leave him, too. He risked everything to save me from my mother only for me to throw my life away a few years later. "I can't remember how…but I think it was here." He lowers his head so his forehead presses against mine. "I don't think I ever really left…not after that night…"

"Well," Viva's mom interjects, placing one hand on her hip as she continues to choke Viva with the other. "Isn't this a touching reunion?"

"I don't know who you are," says my father slowly, the orange light intensifying. "But I won't let anyone hurt my daughter." He and Viva's mother leap forward at the same time; they meet in an explosion of orange, a shrieking tornado of sand encasing their grappling figures.

Through the haze, I see my father's face. "I…remember…" he grunts, glowing so intensely, it hurts to look at him. But I cannot tear my gaze away. He smiles at me one last time "…how much I love my family."

I smile back through my tears. "I remember, too."

A glow intense enough to make the orange light that sometimes coats Viva and I look as faint as candlelight compared to a burning noon sun overtakes my father's body. There is a blaze of light, an explosion of dust; Viva's mother shrieks. Then both of them are gone.

Chapter Twenty-Two

I run a hand down my neck, brushing off some stubborn grains of sand, gasping. I can still feel the pressure of my mom's fingers tightening around my throat. Blinking hard, I can just make out Muerta in the darkness. She's shimmery, almost transparent; I can see the back wall of the cellar through her head. I watch as the cistern behind her transforms into a newer, sleeker model, the pipes replaced with shinier metal. Beside it, there's the washer and dryer that came with the house, and, next to them—

"Francisca," my mom whispers, extending her arms. "Please, sweetheart, please stop fighting me." Her face is drawn but beautiful, her arms thin but seemingly made of solid flesh, not sand. Her long, blonde hair seems to trap all the available light in its tangles as she steps toward me, making her dusty velvet dress seem darker by comparison, red as an old scab. "Come with me."

Slowly, I walk toward her.

"Viva, no!" Muerta cries.

Although the room around us looks like the basement of the new house, I think of the crawl space we had back in San Antonio. It was my favorite place to go during hide and seek because Maria Elena was always too scared of spiders to come looking for me there. Instead, when she exhausted every other hiding spot in the house, she'd go running to Mom, who'd come down with a flashlight and a grin.

I remember the way my mom used to smile, the slightly crooked twist of her lips, higher on the left side than the right. She had blotches on her forehead—acne scars like mine—and the skin on her nose always seemed red and peeling from too much sun. No matter how much time she spent outside, her skin refused to tan. She burned. Sometimes, the skin of her face was several shades darker than the fine blonde hair of her eyebrows, making them stand out like fuzzy caterpillars.

"I love you, Francisca," my mother coos at me now. Her skin is smooth as porcelain, her smile perfectly even. She has an elegant manicure even though her Bloody Mary nail polish was almost always chipped where she bit her nails. Her teeth are toothpaste commercial white, not stained by years of nicotine and diet soda. "We can be happy together."

"No," I say heavily. "We can't."

This perfect mother, the mom I thought I remembered, isn't real. She's the mirror image of the mother I had, the woman who could be cruel, and irrational, and selfish—the mother I forgot.

The clouds of dust that filled the basement when the ghost of Muerta's father lunged at my mom start to coalesce into a version of her even more monstrous than the one that dragged me into the Land of the Dead. Her eyes are empty sockets, oozing darkness. Her mouth gapes. Her red dress is made, not of worn velvet, but rotting flesh. She screeches, reaching for me with crooked claws caked in sand.

I stand my ground.

This olvidado that's been attacking me isn't really my mom, either—just the worst parts concentrated, the ones I refused to let myself think about. I've been repressing the truth ever since she left, but I won't hide from it anymore. It's simple, so simple it almost seems stupid to admit, but I do.

My mother was not a monster. She was not an angel. She was simply my mother.

And I remember her.

I remember how I could always hear her singing in the shower through my bedroom wall. I always thought she had the most beautiful voice in the world, even when she warbled high and off-key.

I remember her eyes narrowing in irritation as I spill off my bike, skinning my knee.

"Balance!" she yelled. "How many times do I have to tell you to balance?"

I remember her grumbling as she slings the crockpot into the backseat of the minivan before my birthday party. "You better hold on tight," she mutters. "I spent all day on that brisket." She sighs and runs a hand up her forehead, smoothing out the beginnings of wrinkles. "Happy birthday to you."

I remember her scolding me for not taking Brisket to the bathroom fast enough and letting him pee on the carpet.

I remember her carefully shampooing my scalp when there was a lice outbreak in my second-grade class and she wrapped my beat-up stuffed turtle in a garbage bag so I could cuddle him safely.

I remember how she told me coffee was illegal if you're under twenty-one so she never had to share with me, not even a sip.

I remember how she always let me ride shotgun if it was just the two of us, even when, in hindsight, it was totally illegal, and the airbags probably would've killed me if she got in an accident.

I remember her singing me to sleep, stroking my hair.

I remember her combing my hair, gritting her teeth while I screamed.

I remember her getting upset when I came home from school with ragged sleeve cuffs because I wouldn't stop chewing them.

I remember her yelling at my first-grade teacher, the one who suggested I get tested for autism.

I remember her yelling at me because Dad was yelling at her. I remember ducking hands, fists, shoes. I remember her crying afterward and holding me so tightly it bruised me even more.

I remember her saying "I love you," but only to the boy I never was.

I don't know what my mom would think of me if she could see me now. I don't know if she would call me Francisca, and I don't even really know what I think about her. Maybe I never will. But I know one thing.

I throw my arms open and pull both versions of my mother into a tight embrace. Tears race down my cheeks. "I remember you."

Slowly, the two olvidados meld into each other, until there's only one body in my arms. I hold her even tighter. After a moment, thin arms close around my back. My mom sighs, a low, deep, rattling sound that seems to come from her core. It's not a pretty sound, but, unlike the gentle coo of her voice earlier, or her inhuman shriek, it feels real. "Thank you," she rasps with her final breath, stroking my cheek with sandpaper hands that dissolve the moment they touch my skin.

I lower my head, closing my eyes. This is what my mom wanted all along: to be let go.

Chapter Twenty-Three

As the ghost of Viva's mother crumbles to dust, a sense of peace washes over me. She was trapped between realms; now, she's able to pass and, by liberating her, Viva has brought us both closer to freedom. I reach for her hand. As our fingers meet, a delicate orange glow pulses between us.

"We're almost there," says Viva, speaking for us both.

I know she can sense it, as I do, in the very air that surrounds us. The howling of the wind has gone quiet. Instead, there is a gentle hush of anticipation. The groaning of the house has ceased. The once-gray light pouring through the cellar door has strengthened, brightened, and it is tinged with the pearl pink of dawn. One memory. Somehow, we know only one more memory awaits us both, and then we'll be able to leave this place.

I nod, but guilt and grief stir in my heart. *There* for Viva means the Land of the Living; for me, there is only death. I have known this all along, but it feels cruel, being made to confront everything I loved in life when I can never get it back, recovering lost parts of myself only to lose them forever.

My father loved me. My father made a terrible sacrifice to protect me. Would I still have chosen to take my life that night if I had known, or had too much been taken from me already? I don't think I would have stayed. Not only had I lost my mother, my sisters, my grandfather, and, so I believed, my father, but I had lost myself, too. Dying was the easiest decision I could have made, the one I thought would reunite me with my family. I did not know what I could have done to recover the girl I was, the Francisca who knew how to have fun, the Francisca who loved to paint and draw, the Francisca who would do anything to protect her friends.

I was once Francisca Viva, too. But I have eaten the bitter fruit of the tree of death, and now I am only Muerta. I made a choice that can never be reversed.

I do not realize that I'm crying until Viva wipes a tear from my cheek.

"One more memory," she says, trying to encourage me.

Instead, her words only make me cry harder.

Viva tentatively pats my shoulder, but it's clear she's unsure of how to help. Her hand is warm and solid; her touch strengthens me. It's almost enough to make me believe I could live, too. I breathe deeply, trying to stem the flow of tears, but a fresh torrent rushes out.

"I don't want to die," I choke out.

Who found me, after that night? Could my father see my hanging feet from the living room window? Was it the first thing he saw in the morning, or did he notice many drinks and hours later, as the sky darkened around me?

Was it Abril, walking past our house on the way to the river? Abril San Miguel. Abril the silent. Abril, my friend. What would she have thought when she saw my body in the tree that took our sisters? I picture her dark eyes obscured by darker hair. I picture her alone. How could I have left her?

How could I have left the sunflower field, the river, the sun, the moon, the sky?

How could I have left *life*?

Life, despite its pain, is a precious, beautiful thing. And I forgot.

I exhale, tilting my face upward so the dawn sun dances in my eyes, in the silvery pools of my tears. I may have forgotten, but at least I was given the chance to remember.

Viva smiles, relieved, when she sees me wipe my eyes. "Come on," she says, putting a hand on my back and scanning the empty cellar. "I don't think I'm gonna find my last memory down here."

I follow her up the ladder into light. As I trail her through the house, whispering olvidados approach us with outstretched hands. Viva stands straight and tall, moving ahead with determination so they part around her, but I pause. Like Pablo Flores-Fuentes, they seem to be encouraged by our journey out of la tierra de los olvidados. One olvidado lets out a hushed breath that almost sounds like my name and straightens the sunflower tucked behind my ear. Then it steps back and melts into the muttering crowd.

When Viva goes upstairs, none of the olvidados go after her. Even so, I hesitate, one foot on the first step, the other on the living room floor. I don't know what to say to them, these faceless figures, or if they can understand me at all, but it seems wrong to leave without acknowledging them. After all, without Viva pushing me forward, I might have become one myself.

"You'll find yourselves, if you look," I say softly. "I did."

Then I turn and follow Viva to the second floor.

She opens the door to the bedroom—hers. Its contents are still in disarray from the olvidado attack earlier, but she remains calm as her eyes scan the mess. She scoops a small, fuzzy, faded orange blanket off the floor, and her eyes glow. In the glow, I see snapshots of memory: a young Viva, maybe seven or eight, with even shorter hair, banging on the door, crying. I hear the rumbling of an automobile in the distance, getting quieter, farther away. Past Viva flings herself onto the bed, pulls the orange blanket over her head, and sobs.

Then Viva closes her eyes; when she opens them, the glow has faded. She sets the blanket on her bed and sits down. She pats the space beside her, and I sit as well.

"Mom was a pageant queen, back in the day," she says, picking at one of the blanket's loose threads. "She always told us about how she was on the homecoming court, and she won some statewide choir competition in high school, and she had a collection of crowns and everything."

She lays back on the bed, closing her eyes again.

"Once she left, Maria Elena started doing pageants, too." Viva sighs, running a hand through her hair. "I was jealous, though I'd rather die than admit it. It didn't seem fair to me, like Maria Elena got everything and I got nothing." Viva starts listing things off on her fingers. "She got to go off with Dad every weekend, she had her own special way to feel close to Mom, she got to be the center of attention—" Viva shakes her head. "No attention from Mom, though, no matter how well she did," she adds in a gentler tone. "I guess all the attention in the world couldn't make up for that." Her eyes open. "We're really not so different."

"What do you think that memory is trying to remind you of?" I ask.

Viva rises and makes her way over to the window, pressing her palms against the glass. "I could have banged on the window," she says slowly. "I remember thinking, if I bang on it hard enough, they'll hear me, and they'll come back." I wonder if she somehow didn't hear my question, but then she says, "That was the day I decided I didn't need either of them, my dad or Maria Elena. That's when I started shutting them out."

I think back to my memory in the cellar, of how I withdrew from my father in suspicion, in horror. "Then we need to reach out to someone, but…" My words trails away as I meet Viva's eyes, my final question—*who?*—unspoken.

Viva grips my hand. "We have each other." She raps her fingers on the windowsill. "But what are we supposed to do?"

Beyond her, beyond the window, the leaves of the orange tree stir gently in the breeze. Light glances off glossy leaves and shining orange skins, illuminating the tips of Viva's curls, making them appear dark brown rather than black. I think of how I stood at that same window with rope in my hands.

All this time, we've been trapped in this house, in our memories. I make my way across the room to stand at Viva's side, and I guide her hands to the windowsill. Our eyes meet, and she gives me a single nod of understanding. Together, we open the window. Instead of letting memories hold us captive, forcing us into forgotten pasts, we must carry the truth within ourselves as we step into the dazzling sunlight of the future.

Orange light radiates from our bodies. I feel weightless; as I take my first tentative step onto a branch of the orange tree, there is no creak of protest. The branch only moves when Viva follows me, sinking beneath her weight. Beneath the glow, her face is bold, solid. Alive.

The leaves whisper around us, like olvidados. Sunlight streams through branches in an emerald haze, brightened by oranges that shine like stars. I turn to Viva and offer her one final smile even as tears fill my eyes. "Viva," I murmur, a name and a promise.

Viva grins back, her own eyes studded with brilliant tears. She grips my hand so hard it aches, so tightly I can feel the lines of her palms pressing against mine. "I'll never forget you."

I tuck my sunflower behind her ear. "Never forget yourself," I tell her. Warm tears caress my cheeks. "No matter how hard it gets, no matter how loudly the tree calls, no matter whose voice it uses—don't listen."

Viva nods gravely, and I know she understands. "I'll live for both of us."

I embrace her. "Thank you."

"Thank *you*," she says, hugging me back.

I let her hold me for a moment, then I rise to my full height. Branches should snag in my hair, but instead, they pass through the space where my head should be. I am light; I am nothing; I am the memory of a memory. I am Francisca Flores, and I now must brave the tree of death, tasting, once and for all, the bittersweetness of its fruit.

I lean back and fall, like Maria Elena.

Chapter Twenty-Four

I watch Muerta fall back, arms outstretched. In the moment before she hits the ground, she disappears in a blaze of orange light.

"Goodbye," I say quietly.

I remember the way she always leapt after me when I rushed into something dangerous. I remember how she used to reach up and touch her sunflower, the one she gave me, whenever she was thinking hard. I remember her questions, her curiosity. I remember her.

"No matter how loudly the tree calls, no matter whose voice it uses—don't listen."

Even full of tears, her eyes were determined when they met mine. She was closer to death than ever, but she never looked more alive.

I think back to that memory of rope around my neck—the memory that was never mine, but could have been. The orange didn't kill me, but I ate it with the understanding that it could have. It was as close to suicide as I've ever been. I could have given up everything I was, every chance to make my life better. I could have died.

Even now, there's a part of me that still thinks about it with some longing. Nothing's changed, really, about my life. My mom is still gone, and now I know it's forever, and she died resenting me. She was so mad, she chased me down beyond the grave to get her revenge. My father's alive, but just as unreachable. The closest he can get to accepting who I am is by ignoring me, pretending I never spoke up in the first place.

How can I want to go back to a life where I'm constantly mocked for being different, when something as minor as wearing barrettes can turn people against me? How can I want to go back to twitching constantly, to having to give up things I love one by one? How can I want to be alive when my own parents don't love me.

I lift my head, staring at the rising sun until my eyes water. How can I want to die when I'll never see another sunrise? I'll lose my chance to ever go to another poetry slam with Tia Lola, to laugh on the phone with Angie and Cat, to sing along to "Francisca" by Luna del Sol, to make things right with Maria Elena, to learn Spanish. They seem like such small things, it's hard to believe they add up to something worth staying alive for. But they do.

I promised Muerta I'd live, and I meant it.

So I flex my fingers, straighten the sunflower behind my ear, and claw my way back to the land of the living. The tree's bark is rough, biting into my hands, and the longer I climb, the hotter it gets, like I'm approaching the sun. I climb for what feels like hours, the tree always extending further into the sky no matter how high I go. Branches threaten to crack beneath my weight, but they never do. They support me. I scale higher and higher, until finally I break through the leaves into dazzling daylight.

I blink back spots, heaving as if I've run a marathon. My hands are calloused and bloody from climbing. My shirt is stuck to my back by sweat. There are twigs in my hair, and a spider crawling up my arm, and I laugh out loud because all these things make me feel *alive*, and that's not something I'm ever going to take for granted again.

When my vision clears, I realize that I'm on the branch that's level with the window to my room. A glance inside is all it takes to confirm that it's the way I left it—aside from the sheets and blanket wadded on the floor by the bed, everything's where it should be. There's no evidence that the place was ever torn apart by olvidados. For a moment, I almost wonder if the whole experience was just a strange dream, but the wind rustles my hair and blows a single dry petal off the sunflower Muerta tucked behind my ear.

I inch my way across the branch and crawl through the open window. I reach out to close it, but a warm breeze that smells like oranges wafts in, making me smile. I leave it open. If I listen carefully, I can almost hear a faraway melody on an accordion.

The music makes me think of my violin. I get down on my stomach and reach under my bed, pulling out the dusty case. As I unzip it, my neck twitches. I hesitate. I know the violin's too small for me now and, even if it wasn't, I probably won't be able to hold the posture. Then, instead of putting the violin between my neck and shoulder, I set it in my lap and pluck three notes. Under my breath, I sing, *"Fran-cis-ca."*

It's not much, but it's music—the first music I've made in a long time. I smile so hard, my cheeks ache.

Maybe I won't be able to play like I used to, but I don't need to. I can find new ways to make the violin work for me, or I can pick up a new instrument, like guitar. Before my mom gave me the violin, before I started trying to make myself as different from Maria Elena as possible, that was what I wanted to play more than anything. I wanted to sing, too.

So, I sing. Just like I did when Muerta and I were scaring olvidados away, I dance, swirling across the room. I fling out my arms and throw back my head and let the notes pour out of me. As I close my eyes, the sunlight streaming through the window turns the darkness behind my eyelids a beautiful orange. Outside, wind rustles the orange tree's leaves, and it sounds like laughter. I wonder if Muerta is finally reunited with the sister she missed so much.

When I finish the song, I sit back down on my bed and, as the mattress slopes toward me, my cell phone bumps against my hip. I flip it open. The battery's low, but there should be enough charge left for one phone call. I think about calling Tia Lola, or Angie, or Cat, but the number I dial is Maria Elena's. She lets it ring for so long, I'm convinced she's going to ignore me. Considering how our last conversation went, I don't blame her, but she picks up on the final ring.

"What do you want?" she asks, the usual perkiness in her voice nowhere to be found.

"Maria Elena, I'm sorry."

There's a pause. "For what?"

I sigh, running a hand through my hair. "For how I acted the other day when—when we heard about Mom." In spite of everything my mom did to me in the Land of the Forgotten and all the painful memories I have of her, my voice still quivers when I talk about her. "I wasn't thinking clearly, so I said something selfish, and stupid, and hurtful, and I'm sorry."

Maria Elena sighs, too, and I picture her trailing a hand down the length of her ponytail—we both have that habit of touching our hair when we're talking about difficult subjects. "I know it must have been hard for you."

"But it's hard for you, too! Mom didn't just belong to me. I—I just—" I take a deep breath. "These past few years, you've been a lot closer to Dad than I have. He doesn't get me, and he's always so proud of you, and your pageants, and stuff, so I kind of…" It's embarrassing to admit out loud, but I get through it. "I guess I claimed Mom in my head to make up for it." I lower my head. "It was stupid."

"No, it makes sense," says Maria Elena, her voice gentle, "and I'm sorry if I've made you feel left out. You've always been so tough and independent, and I really envy that—it doesn't seem like anything gets to you. I don't always understand you, or know the best way to connect." She laughs. "I definitely never would have guessed you were jealous of me."

"Who says I was jealous?" I snap, making her laugh again. This time, I grin, too. "Alright, maybe a little."

"Don't be," says Maria Elena warmly. "If you want to do pageants so badly—"

I gag.

"I can lend you some dresses, give you some pointers in poise—"

"Thanks, but no thanks," I tell her. I pause. "I wouldn't say no if you offered to teach me how to play guitar, though."

"That's a great idea!" Maria Elena exclaims. I can hear the smile in her voice. "Once my summer classes wrap up, I'll drive over to the new house for a week or two and teach you the basics."

"I'd like that."

A rough knock jolts me silent. My dad barks my deadname, then: "I know you're not on that phone again!"

"Talk to you later," I murmur to Maria Elena. "Bye." I snap the phone shut, then startle my dad by opening the door. I tilt my head back to meet his eyes. "Why do you call me that?" I ask quietly.

His eyes narrow. "Call you what? Your *name*?"

"I told you, I'm Francisca."

Dad shakes his head. "You know I don't understand that ABCT community shit."

I raise my voice. "My name is Francisca Luna, and I'm a girl who likes girls. What part of that don't you understand?"

"Don't take that tone with me," my dad warns.

"I'm serious. What do you need me to explain?"

"There's nothing *to* explain. If you want to be gay, that's your choice," he adds, softening his voice in an attempt to compromise. "It'll make your life a hell of a lot harder, but that's on you. My sister's gay, I get it—" he shakes his head "—but you can't just change your gender."

I remember when I first came out to him, and I realized that I was fighting a hopeless battle. The same feelings come over me now—anger, bitterness, defeat. My dad might not be much, but he's the only parent I have left, and even though I know in my heart he's just a stubborn, ignorant man, there's always going to be a part of me that's still a little kid inside, a part that wants my dad to be proud of me.

Then an earlier memory surfaces—me banging on the locked bedroom door while the sound of my dad's car got further away. I remember opening the window with Muerta, sitting with her in the sun. I turn away from my dad to look out the window, and the glossy green of the orange tree's leaves make me think of my Tia Lola's rings. My dad's heart might be a locked door, but the world is full of windows. All I have to do is turn and look.

Then it dawns on me: coming out was never something I did for my dad's sake.

I did it for my own.

I remember myself, small and scared in the dark, curled up on the floor of the laundry room or crouched in the closet. Now, I stand in the light. I have no secrets. I don't have my parents' approval, but even if I never get it, at least I don't have to live in suspense, dreading the day I get caught. *I* know who I am, and that's what matters.

I like slam poetry, and bowling, and quote-unquote "Mexican" food.

I am messy, and reckless, and I wear big, stupid hats.

I am a former violinist, future guitarist, and present-tense singer.

I am the feeling of a bike speeding downhill.

I am the restless rustling of leaves.

I am the moonlight that finds you in your darkest moments.

I am a sunflower that sprouted over the grave of the boy I never was.

I am Francisca Luna Fuentes, and I am unforgettable.

Resources

LGBTQ-specific Mental Health Support and Resources

The Trevor Project
    https://www.thetrevorproject.org/
It Gets Better
    https://itgetsbetter.org/get-help/
Lambda Legal Resources for LGBTQ Youth By State
    https://legacy.lambdalegal.org/sites/default/files/publications/
    downloads/fs_resources-for-lgbtq-youth-by-state_1.pdf

Mental Health/Suicide Prevention Resources

Suicide Prevention Resource Center
    https://sprc.org/
National Alliance on Mental Illness
    https://www.nami.org/

Child Abuse Resources

Childhelp National Abuse Hotline
    https://www.childhelphotline.org/
Covenant House (youth homeless shelters)
    https://www.covenanthouse.org/

<u>Discussion Questions</u>

1.   The novel is set in the year 2010. How would Francisca Viva's story change if she was a modern-day sixteen-year-old? What about Francisca Muerta's?

2.   Despite having very different personalities, the two Franciscas parallel each other in a number of ways. What parallels did you pick up on? What purpose do you think they serve?

3.   Why do you think simply remembering isn't all it takes for the Franciscas to escape la tierra de los olvidados? What, beyond our memories, makes us who we are?

4.   Which of the two Franciscas did you relate to more? Was there another character you felt an even stronger connection with? What drew you to them?

5.   What differences do you notice between the voices of the two Franciscas? What literary techniques are used to create these differences?

6.   Claudesville—or Nuestra Claudia—is a town haunted by its colonial past. What historical events haunt your hometown, or the place you're living now?

7.   Francisca Viva's disinterest in being a "girlie-girl" may seem confusing—or even contradictory—to some readers. What other female characters have you read about that defy gendered stereotypes? Do the ways they break the mold prevent people from accepting them as women or girls?

8. What makes a book a horror novel? How does Francisca and the Forgotten fit within the genre? Are there any expectations it doesn't meet?

9. Both Franciscas have creative hobbies they've left behind over the years. Are there any you've given up or lost interest in as you've gotten older? What would it mean for you to start again?

10. Although Francisca Viva is a lesbian, her story does not involve romance. In what ways is this part of her identity relevant to the book, if at all? Does every facet of a character's identity have to be relevant?

11. How does the book use natural imagery—the description of plants, animals, and landscapes—to set a tone? Do you think it still counts as "natural" imagery when there are also supernatural elements involved, like in the case of the orange tree?

12. The two Franciscas learn to accept that their parents are more complex than the black-and-white versions they feared or idolized. Do you think this new understanding will affect Francisca Viva's relationship with her father? Why or why not?

13. Over the course of the story, several characters have their names forgotten—or ignored. What are some passages about naming that stood out to you? How are names used to give someone power or take it away?

14. What are some reasons a language might be forgotten or "go extinct?" What can be done to keep a language alive?

15. Even in the final chapter, Francisca Viva struggles with suicidal thoughts. What helps her resist? What might have helped Francisca Muerta? What helps you hold on?

Acknowledgements

It only feels right to begin these acknowledgments with Katrina Marie Bryant and Rachael Shaw-Rosenbaum.

I remember Katrina being bubbly and well liked, with blonde hair, sparkling brown eyes, and a binder that had "Got any GRAPES?" written on it in purple marker. That mental snapshot comes from eighth grade English class. In ninth grade, she lost her life to suicide. She has been dead almost as long as she was alive. By the time you read this, that eclipse might have already passed. I hardly knew her, but I remember her. I can only imagine how closely her memory must be held by friends and family to this day.

Rachael and I ran in the same circles. I remember laughing with her at Youth Court picnics and post-debate tournament dinners, where we bonded over being too short and too outspoken. I remember envying and admiring her intellect by turns. Her most cherished ambition was to serve on the Supreme Court, and I can't imagine anyone meeting her and doubting that she could. Her suicide came just before what would have been the end of her freshman year at Yale, where she was repeatedly denied mental health leave. Her loss makes me wonder how impoverished our world and our histories are by suicide, by a callous, capitalist culture that forces its best and brightest to burn out the fastest.

On a more conventional note, I want to thank my friends and publishers, Josh Smyser and Alex Hale, who are very fortunately still alive. Being a published author has been my dream since I was five years old, and I couldn't have asked for a better team to help me realize it. Additionally, I'm grateful for all the other amazing people I met at Western Colorado University: Kevin J. Anderson, Allyson Longueira, and my wonderful cohort.

I also want to appreciate the many professors, teachers, and mentors who have helped me on this journey, from Julia O'Malley, who recently gave me querying advice, to Ron Kuka and Claire-Agnes Werkiser back at UW-Madison, all the way back to David Vano and Temperance Tinker in high school. My boss, Jenny Dickinson, also deserves mention for providing a supportive work environment, which was instrumental for me in finding the time to finish my first novel and later attend grad school.

It goes without saying that I'm thankful for my family, but I'm sure they'll want me to say it anyway, so here we go. I'm grateful to my siblings, Scott and Erica Santaella, for reminding me that there's more to life than depression—sometimes, there's depression and bad memes. If that's not worth holding on for, I don't know what is.

My grandparents, Mike and Bernadette Moyer and Juan and Lucy Aragon, have always encouraged my writing, and I'm lucky to have them. My grandmother Pipa (Elva Santaella) has been gone for many years, but her kind, comforting presence was a great blessing in my childhood, and she will always be remembered with love.

My parents have given me invaluable support, and this book wouldn't exist without them. My mom, Melissa Moyer, taught me to love writing; my dad, Mario Santaella, taught me the importance of a strong work ethic; my stepmom, Julie Santaella, taught me the value of a good education. Thank you for teaching by example and always having faith in me.

Finally, I want to acknowledge any thoughts you, the reader, may have that mirror Katrina's, or Rachael's, or mine, or Francisca's. There is no detail about you too small to matter. A word, a gesture, a paper you scribbled on—things you've already forgotten—are even now being remembered by people you know, or knew, or met just once and never again. Your presence extends so far beyond the confines of your mind, regardless of what it tells you in your darkest moments. You might be spoken of for centuries to come. You might be the girl someone sees in the hallway. Either way, you are worth remembering.

About the Author

Solaris Santaella is an author, editor, and creative force to be reckoned with. With a BA in English from the University of Wisconsin-Madison and an MA in Publishing from Western Colorado University, Solaris is determined to confront inequality on and off the page. Particularly within genre fiction, they hope to create space for stories featuring dazzling other worlds that aren't afraid to tackle the issues marginalized people face in this one. They were awarded a Eudora Welty Fiction Thesis Prize in 2016 and a Writers of the Future Honorable Mention in 2024. Solaris currently resides in Anchorage, Alaska, with strong family ties to the American Southwest.

You can connect with Solaris online on their website (solarissantaella.com) or YouTube channel (Solaris Santaella).